Crossing the Bravo, for Pueblito

When rancher, bully and wife-beater Clayton T. Pallister is murdered, the tragedy has its compensations. For his wife, Rosie, the harsh years are over, the Rolling P ranch is hers and her young son Warren looks forward to a life away from his powerful father's stifling rules.

Then, only days after the funeral, a young woman rides across the Bravo from Mexico and everything is thrown into disarray. Not only is doubt cast on the legality of Rosie's inheritance but the young woman has brought in her wake two ruffians who are clearly up to no good. They are soon followed by a Mexican landowner who is keen to get a foothold on the rich soil of southern Texas.

So, as Clayton T. Pallister's mysterious past is resurrected and the fight for the Rolling P becomes ever more complicated and violent, Warren realizes that he has a fight on his hands that can only be settled when all factions come together in a blaze of gunfire.

Crossing the Bravo, for Pueblito

Jim Lawless

A Black Horse Western

ROBERT HALE · LONDON

© Jim Lawless 2010
First published in Great Britain 2010

ISBN 978-0-7090-8976-6

Robert Hale Limited
Clerkenwell House
Clerkenwell Green
London EC1R 0HT

www.halebooks.com

Typeset by
Derek Doyle & Associates, Shaw Heath
Printed and bound in Great Britain by
CPI Antony Rowe, Chippenham and Eastbourne

PROLOGUE

Though it was already early fall, the heat was unrelenting. The midday sun beating on the tiled roof of the shabby adobe cottage in the village of Pueblito, Mexico, turned the interior into an oven. The old woman lying on the bed, the single blanket pushed down to her waist, was glistening with perspiration. The thin nightdress was sticking to her body. Her eyes were dull. They closed each time her daughter used a damp cloth to cool her face, and on those occasions a faint smile flickered about her lips.

The younger woman, in her mid-forties, dark haired and slim in a simple shift dress, was frowning. She was attentive, filled with compassion and a deep understanding of her mother's frail condition. But today her thoughts were elsewhere. During her ministrations her eyes flickered constantly to the folded newspaper that had been brought across the border from Laredo, Texas, and which now lay alongside her mother on the bed. At last, unable to contain herself any longer, she voiced her uncertainty.

'I do not understand,' she said softly. 'This . . . this thing that has happened. I cannot see how it affects me – how it can work to my advantage. To our advantage.'

'I will not be here, so in that way it does not concern me,' the old woman said, and for an instant she closed her eyes. When she opened them again, they were wet with unshed tears. 'But it will work to your advantage because when you show yourself to these people, and in the manner of your approach, an illusion will be created: it will appear that what happened twenty years ago did not happen, and consequently what went before it has not changed.'

'But it has. Almost twenty years ago the most important thing that we had was taken away, and everything else became nothing.'

'But now you will make it something again. For a few days. For the time it takes.'

A tall man entered the adobe as she was speaking. The sunlight flooded in behind him, bringing with it the smell of hot dust and rank water and the sicklier scent of cactus. The man's appearance suggested he was as old as the woman but, while she was frail and clearly close to death, he was upright and bursting with good health. Beneath grey, bushy eyebrows, his dark eyes gleamed as he placed a hand on the younger woman's shoulder.

'She is right,' he said softly to his daughter, 'but to

pursue this claim we have to leap into action now, today. We must ride to the Bravo—'

'No.'

The young woman's voice was strained, and she pressed the back of her hand to her mouth as she looked down at her mother.

In that instant the man understood her concern, her reluctance.

'All right,' he said. 'We wait – but then, when it is over—'

'You ride across the Bravo into Texas,' the old woman said. Her eyes were on the man who was her husband, and they, as much as her words, were sending him a message.

'You make sure you pursue this,' she continued, her voice fading almost to a whisper. 'You will be doing it for our village, for Pueblito. More importantly, you will be doing this for Maria. Nevertheless, you must be careful. Nothing is straightforward. The prize is enormous. Señor Gonzales has tried—'

'He was the first to try, but he and his caballeros are going about it the wrong way and he does not have the advantage we enjoy; he does not know what we know, does not realize what we plan,' the old man said. 'Be assured, we will get there before him, with a claim that is legally incontestable; he will watch helplessly as we snatch that prize from under his nose.'

'For Pueblito and for Maria – you will do that?'

7

'For Pueblito, and for Maria,' he said forcefully and, as he said this, there was a catch in his voice and he was already reaching blindly for her veined hand.

By sunset that night, the old woman was dead.

Her husband, the white-haired old man who was upright and vigorous, buried her at daybreak. The whole village turned out, gathering on the slopes of the village's small cemetery to pray for her soul.

Two men stood at the back of the crowd. They were bareheaded, their heads respectfully lowered. But from that position their eyes were active: they were watching the old man, and his daughter.

A short while later, when the villagers had returned to their homes or their places of work, the man and his daughter gathered together the supplies they would need – in the man's case this included a pistol and an ancient rifle – and with the sun still a pale promise to the east they mounted their horses and turned them towards the Rio Bravo del Norte and the Texas town of Laredo.

One hour later, dust was kicked up to drift like thin mist in the morning light as two riders rode up the stony slope of Pueblito's only street. They were the men who had watched covertly on the outskirts of the mourners. Their names were Herrera and Delgado. Both were raw-boned and unshaven, dressed in shabby clothing, with soiled bandannas encircling their throats and dark, sweat-stained hats pulled low. Many silver conchos glittered, reflecting the intense light of the rising sun. That same light caught the cold steel of the men's rifles, the pistols they carried at their hips; the flash of teeth as the taller of the two grinned at his companion.

They rode past the house where the old woman had died, and when they reached the edge of the village, their horses' hoofs trod the same trail as that taken earlier by the man and his daughter. The two men rode without haste. They were an hour behind those they followed, but they knew that an even pace would steadily decrease the distance between them.

After that, it was simply a matter of keeping them in sight, without themselves being seen.

ONE

'A crystal chandelier is what I want,' Clayton T. Pallister said, his rich baritone voice filled with self importance. 'This chunk of worm-eaten timber'll do for now, but I hear tell Charlie Goodnight up in the Palo Duro has ordered one of those crystal contraptions from New York. Play my cards right, I can get in ahead of him then make sure he knows about it. That'll be another feather in my cap.'

While talking he was leaning back in his chair, hands laced across his stomach as he gazed up at the massive wagon wheel that hung horizontally almost directly over his head. It was suspended by a single rope attached to its hub. Polished brass oil lamps were affixed at regular intervals around its iron-bound rim. Their mellow light cast a warm glow over the dark sheen of the dining table, the china crockery and silver knives and forks and the three people partaking of their evening meal. Just outside the circle of light, expensive furniture stood against walls hung with oil paintings in gilt frames.

The eight-foot oak refectory table was set lengthwise across the room. Clayton T. was sitting at the centre of one long side, facing the window. His son, Warren sat at the head of the table. From that position he was able to lift his gaze to look at an oil painting of his father that hung on the wall directly behind his mother, Rosie. Clayton T.'s wife, blue-eyed and still slim though her fair hair was streaked with grey, was sitting at the opposite end of the table to her son.

Watching his father, twenty-year-old Warren Pallister had great difficulty stopping his lip from curling. He held the burly, florid rancher in contempt, and was reluctant to blurt a scathing retort only because of his mother's presence at the table. As always, she was watching and listening to her husband without any expression on her face. She, Warren knew, would not make an observation of any kind. However harmless her words, Clayton T. Pallister would almost certainly find something wrong in them and take her to task later when they had retired to their bedroom at the rear of the big house – either by the flailing use of harsh words, or by using the palms of his hard hands on her slender frame.

'Flashy fitments can come when fall round-up's done and the cattle safely driven up the Goodnight-Loving trail to the Kansas railhead,' Warren said, unable to keep the sarcasm out of his voice as he went on to speak the unpalatable truth. 'Goodnight was a pioneer. He's now the richest, most powerful rancher up in the Panhandle – a thousand miles to the North. The Rocking P's on the San Miguel Creek – Goodnight's probably never heard of it. Bigfoot's our nearest town and it's little more than a village; it's another forty-mile ride to San Antonio. You're a fool to try to match Goodnight. You should be more concerned about competition from ambitious upstarts crowding you from closer to home—'

'Not match him,' Pallister said, ignoring the advice. 'I'll better him. And I'll get there—'

'If somebody doesn't get you first.'

Pallister glared.

'What the hell does that mean?'

Warren made a small exclamation of disbelief.

'Don't tell me you know nothing of your own reputation?'

'Everybody's envious of a successful man,' Pallister said, his chin jutting. 'That's part of the price I pay.'

'Nonsense. I'm talking about hate, not envy. The hatred of men you've ridden over rough-shod, others you've ruined by driving them off barren land they were slowly bringing to life.'

'My land,' Pallister said.

'You didn't use it then, you don't use it now. And the success of this ranch depends more on the men you hire than on your own efforts. During the past year you've been away frequently, sometimes for two weeks out of every month. You never say where

12

you've been, or what you've been doing.'

'The men I hire are experienced ranch hands. Ranch hands are directed by the foreman. The foreman operates according to the dictates of the ranch owner: me. The ranch owner is responsible for dealing with, among other things, the business's financial affairs. That, and any number of other important matters, can take me away from the ranch—'

'For days on end—'

'Yes. And until you decide that you want to be an active part of that business – instead of just going through the motions – that's all you need to know, all you're *going* to know.'

Pallister pushed his chair back, picked up a crystal wine decanter and filled his glass. He looked at his wife. Her smile was gentle as she shook her head. His lips clamped to a thin line.

'Drink it,' he said, leaning along the length of the table to splash wine into her glass. 'With luck it'll take that sour look off your face.'

She blinked, flashed a look down the table at her son then managed a small shake of the head as she saw he was about to speak up in her defence.

'Isn't that a rider I can hear approaching?' Rosie Pallister said softly.

'I hear horses, restless cattle, I hear a guitar being played badly and I hear men laughing,' Pallister said, as he sat down. 'For God's sake, woman, this is a working ranch you're living on.'

'Laughter is mostly absent from this room, this house,' Warren said, and his eyes were challenging his father. 'As for a rider, Ma's right, because I can hear someone. But apart from Jake Furnival – who is playing his guitar with considerable skill – all the hands are in bed, playing cards, or talking about the start of the round-up. And as you have no friends, and no business associate would be riding up to the house at this time, I think she's right to be apprehensive.'

'What do you mean? You know I've got friends.'

'Sure you have,' Warren said. 'They're men like you. They're your friends because nobody else will be seen associating with them. You've formed a small, tight circle, and all those within it are despised by decent men.'

He glanced towards the window, saw the lamplight glowing in the bunkhouse, the thin cold sliver of moon – and a barely discernible movement, a faint glint of reflected light.

'Maybe,' he said, frowning, 'you're expecting one of those toadies who cluster around you waiting for crumbs—'

'What I'm expecting,' Pallister cut in, 'is a successful fall gather, a successful drive north, massive profits from a successful sale. Then we'll see about Charlie Goodnight and his heroic exploits, his money, his fancy crystal chandeliers—'

He got no further. Even as anger boiled over and his face became suffused with blood, a shot rang out.

Glass shattered in the big window. Warren ducked, then dived sideways as glittering fragments flew like shrapnel. The bullet hissed across the room and thudded into the rear wall. On its way there was a faint snick. The rope holding the massive wagon wheel with its cargo of oil lamps parted. As Warren watched in horror from the floor there seemed to be an eerie pause during which nothing moved. Then the big wheel dropped vertically. On it's way down the edge of the iron-bound rim struck Clayton T. Pallister on the head. An oil lamp shattered, flared. Blood spurted as Pallister's scalp split. Driven down by the huge weight landing on his head, he toppled backwards, taking his chair with him. As the huge wagon wheel crashed on to the refectory table, then settled on Pallister's already still form, glasses and plates exploded into glittering shards. Dark red wine spilled out to mingle with the blood pouring from the dead rancher's head on to the expensive Persian carpet.

TWO

Dawn was a thin slash of bright light on the horizon, a thread of gold that would expand across the vast Texas plains on the eastern side of the Bravo. To Jesus Gonzales, as he walked silently off carpeted floors and on to the broad veranda fronting his hacienda to the north of Nuevo Laredo, Mexico, it was at once the promise of riches to come.

It was three days after the death of Clayton T. Pallister.

Gonzales stood looking towards the great, rolling river, over grassland damp with dew and, as he smoked the first cigar of the day, he knew that the waiting was over. The time had arrived when he, Jesus Gonzales, would get a foothold on the rich Texas cattle country. Raulo Chavez had kept him up to date with developments at the Murphy homestead. The two women had been undecided, but the sudden and *lamentable* death of Pallister – Gonzales took the cigar from his mouth and grinned at the cynical thought – was sure to make their minds up for them. Reliable, relentless Raulo would see to that. The sisters were old, rich, and their eyes were set on the stars. They would buy the Rocking P from Rosie Pallister, the dead man's widow, and at once they would be out of their depth.

When the excitement was over, the realization of what they had taken on would in itself be enough to overwhelm them. On top of that they would see a sudden change in Raulo. He would no longer be a friend and adviser, but a hard man sneering at their foolishness. He would warn them that they had made enemies, and point to the death of Clayton T. Pallister as an example of what could happen.

And then, he, Jesus Gonzales would arrive. He would have with him two men chosen for their appearance: former bandits, they were always ready to slip into their old, bad ways. One, Blanco, had a scarred face, and eyes that were inhuman. The other, Rubio, was blessed with clawed hands that moved restlessly, constantly, and invariably instilled terror into those with vivid imaginations who watched, and wondered.

Those two women, they will give up the Rocking P as swiftly as they took on the burden, Gonzales thought. They would watch him and his bandoleros ride on to their poor homestead before they had time to move into the richer premises built many years ago by Clayton T. Pallister. And when he, Gonzales, rode in, it would be too late. It would be all over for them.

Gonzales had been unable to persuade Pallister to sell. For twelve months, on the rancher's frequent visits, he had been plied with drink and offered female company, yet still the man had continued to hold out. Even if he, Gonzales, had succeeded in turning the man's mind, there would have been legal difficulties to overcome. A Mexican would always encounter difficulties; a Mexican with a past shrouded in darkness would quite possibly have been classed as an undesirable, and the deal blocked; in combination, the barriers to the sale would have been insurmountable.

But now, circumstances had changed. The man had refused to be swayed, so he had been removed. Rosie Pallister would sell to the Murphys. Bypassing legal channels, Gonzales would offer Meg Murphy and her sister a sum of money, in cash, far less than they had paid for the Rocking P – and they would accept.

Even if they did not, Gonzales thought contentedly, the Pallister spread would be his. One way or another, by reasonably fair means or by the use of any other methods that were required, he would take the Rocking P from the Murphy sisters.

That same day, three days after his father's funeral, Warren Pallister left the Rocking P a little after noon and rode into Bigfoot.

He had spent the morning supervising preparations

for the fall round-up. Several of the extra men who would work the gather with the Rocking P hands were struggling to start their own spreads elsewhere, and were grateful for the wages they got from spring and fall round-ups. They had been riding in from all directions. Each man had a string of six horses in the Rocking P's cavvy. Those arriving with time to spare had used the week prior to the round-up to get their horses once again accustomed to saddle and rider.

When Warren rode out, straw boss Jack Fisher had the men gathered around him as he assigned tasks for the first day, while cook Charlie Longstreet smirked as he tried to drown Fisher's words by noisily loading pans on to the chuck wagon.

Just three men were remaining at the Rocking P: Jake Furnival had a twisted knee – which didn't prevent him from playing his guitar; Al Rickard was recovering from a bad fever; and Bony Park was a former wrangler, too old for range work but part of the scenery for so long Rosie was reluctant to let him go.

There was some livestock to be tended to, and those tasks would be handled by the three men left behind – the sick, the lame and the lazy, as big Jack Fisher put it good-naturedly. But that was about the total of the activity: for at least the next two weeks, the Rocking P would be a virtual ghost ranch.

Bigfoot was half-an-hour's ride to the north. More village than town, it had a scattering of business premises straggling crookedly along both sides of an unusually wide, dusty thoroughfare. It was as if settlers had arrived, set up homes and businesses where they'd unloaded their wagons, and only later realized that what they were creating was a permanent township without shape.

When Warren rode in, that wide thoroughfare was almost deserted. The early fall weather was unusually hot. It was a little past midday, and Bigfoot's citizens were enjoying a lengthy siesta. Dust drifted on the warm breeze as a lone wagon trundled ahead of Warren's big roan. He pulled the horse back to a slow walk to let the wagon and oxen get clear. Then he pushed on past Mick Loder's livery barn, tied the roan to the pole in front of the small jail and went inside.

Marshal Brent Coolidge was a tall, lean figure behind the desk – a middle-aged man with thinning fair hair, content to cool his heels in a town off the beaten track while he waited for retirement. Another man with a sweeping black moustache was leaning forward in his chair as he talked to Coolidge. His name was George Gelert. He was a part-time deputy where none was actually required, a man without gainful employment who peppered his back trail with tall stories and foolishly believed his own image was improved by that reflected glory. He broke off talking as Warren walked in, and sat back.

'Warren,' Coolidge said. 'I thought you'd be busy for the next couple of weeks.'

'The men will. Jack Fisher's a capable foreman.

Out there on the gather I'd only get in the way.'

Coolidge nodded slowly.

'So what brings you to town?'

Warren smiled. 'Don't you mean what brings me here to your humble office?'

Coolidge shrugged, waited.

'All right,' Warren said. 'I came to see what progress you've made in the search for my pa's killer.'

The man with the sweeping moustache laughed softly. Coolidge rocked back in his chair, laced his hands behind his head.

'Where do you suggest we start? The man wasn't exactly popular. If we tackle everyone who bore him a grudge—'

'How about talking to people known to have threatened him? Danny Fargo who runs that horse outfit out on Shot Pine Creek. The Kirk brothers, trappers working the timber back of Dark Ridge. And I'd pay particular attention to Meg Murphy and her sister. They can handle rifles, both of them, and whoever killed Pa pulled off one hell of a tricky shot.'

'Empty threats are worthless. And what could any of them hope to gain?'

Warren frowned. 'I don't know. Satisfaction? The same kind of relief you get from pulling an aching tooth?'

'That's not a lot, when weighed against the crime. No monetary value there. No financial benefits. You really think any of those people would kill for such trivial reasons?'

'I think all of them would, given the opportunity and the belief that they had an even chance of getting away with it.'

'If that's true, what about the man who stands to gain the most?'

This was George Gelert. He was leaning back in his chair, long legs stretched out, thumbs hooked manfully in his belt. His mild, dreamer's eyes were fixed on Warren Pallister.

'Ah.' Warren nodded slowly. 'I wondered when we'd get around to that.'

'If the will reads as I expect, your mother's the new owner of Rocking P,' Brent Coolidge said. 'She'll rely on you entirely, so overnight you'll go from working for a man you hated to being the big boss with responsibility for a heap of money sitting in the Bigfoot bank.'

'Aren't you forgetting something?'

'Am I? You tell me.'

'My pa was killed with a shot from a rifle, fired from the yard. How could I commit such a murder if I was there, in the room, when he died?'

'You never heard of a hired gun?'

'Sure. But why hire a man to pull off a shot like that, when my pa could have been downed much easier any time he was out riding the open range? By me, if it comes to that.'

'Yeah, but it was you who talked about satisfaction,' George Gelert said. 'If you hated the man enough, I can't think of anything more satisfying than sitting there with a glass of fine wine in your hand as you watch him die.'

'In front of his wife? My own mother?'

'The way I hear it,' Brent Coolidge said, 'one of the reasons you hated that man is because, for the whole time they were married, Clayton T. Pallister got pleasure from mistreating that woman. If you hated him, how'd you think she felt? My guess is she'd be cheering right there alongside you.'

'Wrong. She was regularly mistreated, yes, but Ma's too soft-hearted ever to wish anyone any harm.'

'Fair enough. But all that does is bring us back to you.'

Still standing, Pallister shook his head in disbelief.

'I don't know why, but it's becoming clear that's the way you'd like this to end: me taken into San Antonio for a quick trial then convicted of murder. So – are you arresting me?'

'Is that a confession?'

Pallister swore under his breath, then turned on his heel.

'Alex Crow's a good lawyer, and he's always acted for our family. As well as calling here, I'm in town to discuss the will. Maybe I'd better talk to him about defending me when I get charged with patricide.'

On his way out, he slammed the door hard. He couldn't be sure, but he thought he heard both men laughing.

*

23

Alex Crow's office was across the street from the jail. He'd once told Warren that men like Brent Coolidge, steeped in the tradition of their office, believed a badge gave them unlimited power. Being overlooked – being, as it were, under the eagle eye of a competent and observant lawyer – was considered by Crow to be an excellent restraint. Even though, when forced to face reality, he would grudgingly admit that the lawman and the lawyer in Bigfoot were two ageing professionals who relied heavily on each other as they plodded towards the end of their careers in a somnolent backwater.

'Nevertheless, it makes that Coolidge feller think twice before twisting the law so it points in his direction,' he had said, and the grin that he'd flashed at that time was again twitching his lips when Warren walked in.

'A sad time,' he said, rising to shake hands. 'Take no notice of the smile, young feller. I tend to find most things amusing, and I've just been talking to a man who wants a divorce because his wife's fed him the same meal five times a week for the past ten years!'

The lawyer was short and fat, and spidery laughter lines radiated from his wide mouth and his sparkling blue eyes. He had a habit of running a hand across his bald head, frowning as he did so as if unable to believe his hair had gone. He did it as Warren watched – a quick sweep across naked skin – then returned to his desk and flopped into a leather swivel chair.

'So, Warren, what brings you here today? I saw you come out of the jail, so is this a complaint about our marshal's tardiness in looking for your pa's killer?'

'Going there was a waste of time,' Pallister said, moving to the chair Crow indicated. 'But the talk we had has made me very keen to see Clayton T. Pallister's will, and where Ma figures in it.'

'Nowhere, is the simple answer,' Kay said. 'And that's because there ain't none.'

'No will?'

'That's right.'

'Then who inherits? Who's the new owner of the Rocking P?'

'On paper – or according to law – that would be Rosie Pallister. Your ma. Estate goes to next of kin, and so far it looks like she's it.'

'Glory be.' Pallister smiled. 'In a way that gets me off the hook, though Coolidge doesn't see it that way.'

Crow pursed his lips.

'That's because the hook's got many barbs, son. Your pa got murdered and that's him out of the way for good. If she's next of kin then your ma would inherit the spread, but everybody knows you'll be running the show. Any lawman keen for a conviction would point that out. Tie in your dislike of the man for the way he mistreated Rosie, and there's be a damn good case for you being behind the killing.'

'Behind it as in hiring a gunman to do my dirty work?' Warren nodded. 'Maybe so, but they'd have a hard time proving it. Besides. . . .'

He trailed off, frowning. Alex Crow waited, then took a cigar out of a humidor and reached for matches.

'Besides . . . what?'

'You've been up to the house, had dinner with Clayton T. Where does he always sit?'

'That's an easy one. He sits at the head of the table. And why he does it is well known: he takes that seat so he can gaze at that huge, flattering oil painting he had done of himself.'

'So how did he get killed by a wagon wheel falling on his head? That wheel was hanging over the centre of the table.'

'Well, I'll be damned,' Crow marvelled. 'You're right – and that's where you usually sit – isn't it?'

As Warren nodded, Crow frowned thoughtfully. Clearly intrigued, obviously considering the many possible implications of what he had said, he remained silent for a few moments, then struck a match and lit the cigar. As blue smoke swirled, he looked narrow-eyed at Warren Pallister.

'Are you saying that wagon wheel was meant for you?'

'I don't know. It's doubtful. At the Rocking P I'm insignificant, a young kid without too much interest in what goes on.'

'But the new seating arrangement raises some interesting questions, doesn't it? How did the change come about? Did you ask Clayton T. to change seats?

26

Did your ma suggest it? Or did he do it all by himself?'

'Again, I don't know. When I walked into the room, the meal was on the table. Pa was sitting in my usual chair, Ma was in her place and so I walked to the vacant chair at the head of the table.'

'But you see what I'm getting at? And the intriguing point is that no outsider – and especially nobody setting out to investigate the killing – could possibly know why your pa moved to the fatal chair. They're going to have to take your word for what happened and, in the circumstances, you can't be trusted.'

Warren frowned. 'Why not?'

'Because if it wasn't Clayton T.'s idea, then someone must have arranged it. That has to be you, or your ma – or the two of you working together.'

'You know that's not true.'

'Do I? There was nobody else in the house, nobody except the three of you sitting down to dinner. Who the hell else could it have been?'

'Christ, Alex—'

'Easy, now. I'm simply pointing out how it looks to an outsider, and how a prosecutor might put it to a jury.'

For a few moments there was an uncomfortable silence. Warren knew that Alex Crow was looking at what had happened through a lawyer's eyes, and from that perspective it was clear to Warren that he and his mother could be in deep trouble. Marshal

Brent Coolidge was already suspicious, and it could only be a matter of hours or days before he was pushed into action by the sheriff over at San Antonio. Unless Warren could come up with some answers, and fast, he was going to be asked a number of questions to which he had no answer.

Rosie, too, was going to face an uncomfortable time. Despite his frequent absences, Clayton T. Pallister had built the Rocking P ranch into a thriving business. As the beneficiary, Rosie Pallister. . . .

Beneficiary. Warren frowned. Then, fist clenched, he tapped his teeth thoughtfully with his thumbnail as he thought back over the lawyer's words.

'You said,' he said slowly, 'that *so far it looks like she's it.* Meaning next of kin. Then you said—'

'If she's next of kin, then your ma would inherit the spread.'

'Right.' Warren nodded. 'I don't like the sound of those words, Alex. So far it looks like. If she's next of kin. She would inherit. What exactly are you trying to say?'

Alex Crow blew smoke from his nostrils, then spent a few moments studying the tip of his cigar. When he looked up, in his bright grey eyes there was a look of compassion.

'What I was trying to say without actually putting it into words was that it seems there's some doubt. Rosie should be next of kin. However, over the past few days I've heard . . . rumours. If they turn out to be true – for reasons which at the moment I'm keeping to myself – then neither you nor your ma are going to see a cent of Pallister's money.'

THREE

Warren Pallister stayed in town for the rest of that day. For most of the time he was deep in thought.

He ate a wonderful fry-up in the diner owned by one of Rosie's closest friends, saw nothing in her face – even though she had watched him leave Alex Crow's office – to suggest that she was uneasy, or was hiding anything from him. He lingered awhile when he'd finished his meal, giving her every opportunity to talk to him confidentially, but left when it was clear she either knew nothing or wasn't prepared to talk.

After that he called in at the livery barn to make sure the hostler, Mick Loder, had followed his instructions about the care of his horse. The windmill outside the barn from which the horse trough and much of the town got its water was still sagging drunkenly, the broken vanes turning with a continuous squeal of dry bearings. The town council – a three-man panel – had for months been figuring out how to finance a new windmill, so far with no luck.

Warren gave the rickety legs a kick on his way out, splashed water on his face from the very bottom of the trough, then took what seemed to be a preordained course to the bar in the Wild Horses saloon. It was dusk. He was tired, and confused. Strong drink was unlikely to help him think, but the one thing it could do was dull the feeling of pain. He felt . . . what? Betrayed? Or simply bewildered? Quite possibly both but, as he took his first taste of saloonist Barney Kay's finest whisky, he consoled himself with the knowledge that he should also be highly sceptical.

Alex Crow could be wrong. And even if he was right about the rumours – whatever they were – the rumours themselves could be without substance.

Barney Kay, lugubrious, and with wire glasses perched on the end of his thin nose, was behind the bar polishing a glass that was already gleaming. He was watching Warren with a speculative expression in his shrewd eyes.

'You see that feller's been watching you?'

Warren turned, looked around the almost empty room, then faced the bar again to see Kay rolling his eyes.

'Earlier,' Kay said. 'Most of the day, in fact. Hell, Bigfoot's got just the one street, and he was directly across it when you left Alex. Then hanging around again when you went in Caroline's place to eat. And if I'm right, he was in the livery barn when you were talking to Mick about your horse.'

'Him?' Warren downed his drink, planted the empty glass on the bar. 'He was over in one of the stalls tending to a roan looked like it was lame. Didn't once glance my way.'

'Wouldn't, would he?' Kay said, refilling Warren's glass. 'If he was watching you – for some reason – he wouldn't want you to catch him at it.'

'Recognize him?'

Kay shook his head.

'There you are then,' Warren said. 'A stranger in a town this small would naturally look awkward, unsure—'

'This'un looked the exact opposite: too damn sure of himself. And dangerous. Smug look on his face. Kept hitchin' his gun-belt. I swear he was so damned pleased with himself he was almost licking his lips.'

'You see a lot,' Warren said, 'for a man who works indoors.'

Kay sighed. 'In my job, a man notices things. Now, if you think I'm talking nonsense, that's your affair, but if I were in your shoes, I'd be watching my back.'

'Has this got something to do with my pa's death?'

'In what way?'

'I'm asking you.'

'And I'm wondering which direction your thoughts are heading. I know how your pa died. If you're thinking this feller watching you has something to do with that, then my advice stands:

watch your back.'

Without waiting for Warren's answer, Kay drifted away to serve a man waiting at the other end of the bar. Frowning, Warren turned, hooked his elbows on the bar and looked broodingly towards the windows. They were bare, uncurtained, the glass coated with street dust. Seen through them, the oil lamps on the other side of the street wore haloes. Warren could see several horses at the hitch rail and, further away, the rectangular glow that marked the livery barn's open doors.

Nothing unusual. Nobody – as far as he could see – hanging about watching and waiting. But then, why should there be? The day had started off normally, but, as soon as he had ridden into town it had gone downhill. Yet none of the bad news he had heard was truly bad, because none of it had been substantiated. Alex Crow had listened to rumours, Barney Kay had watched a stranger who was doing nothing wrong.

Warren Pallister took a deep breath. He looked at his glass, saw it was still half full, and placed it on the bar with a grimace of distaste. Then, nodding to Barney who had resumed his glass polishing, he headed for the doors.

The evening air was warm, the breeze carrying the scent of sage too gentle to stir the dust of the street. Few of the business premises were lit. Alex Crow's office was in darkness. A lamp glowed in the window of the jail, suggesting Brent Coolidge was working late. Caroline was locking the door of her café – she looked across, saw Warren and waved.

Smiling to himself, Warren stepped away from the saloon's door.

He didn't hear the shot. All he knew was that a tremendous blow struck him on the shoulder. Suddenly there was a hissing in his ears. He was knocked backwards. He hit the door hard with the back of his head. Then he was down and looking up at the sky. The stars seemed to shimmer. He could hear his own pulse, now roaring in his ears; the thunder that was almost a vibration and could have been the drum of a horse's hoofs. As blackness engulfed him he thought he saw a brilliant flash, heard another roar that seemed to go on and on, assailing his ears. Then there were no sounds and, as he sank weightlessly into oblivion, every one of the stars was extinguished.

FOUR

The town was as quiet as the grave when Warren Pallister unsteadily made his way back to main street from the doctor's surgery: a run-down cabin with a ramshackle gallery, set in scrub on the edge of Bigfoot.

A bitter smile curled his lips at the imagery in his thought because, if there had been any feeling at all, then his drift into unconsciousness had indeed felt uncomfortably like the end of his life. A cold grave had been altogether too close, he realized. The bullet had hit him in the left shoulder. According to the bespectacled doctor – who had worked on him with a stinking, smoking corn-cob pipe jutting from his unshaven jaw – if it had struck six inches lower Warren's final journey would have been on a board up to Boot Hill. As it was he was unsteady on his feet, the bandaged wound was aching badly enough to bring the sheen of cold sweat to his face, and a hundred yards from Brent Coolidge's jail he was forced to turn his head from the plank walk to vomit in the street.

Even then, without fully admitting it, he knew that the cause of the sickness welling up in his throat was in his mind as well as in his body. The part of it that was tormenting his thoughts was so awful that he was rejecting it each time it surfaced. Brent Coolidge had planted the seed when discussing the identity of Clayton T. Pallister's killer, and now the bullet that had ripped the soft flesh of Warren's shoulder led directly to a question he could scarcely contemplate, never mind answer: if he was the only man likely to benefit from the death of Clayton T, and he was now the gunman's target, who was the most likely person to be behind the shooting?

Knowing that there was only one possible answer, yet blanking his mind to that thought, Warren spat the sickness from his mouth and rested there, bent over with his hands on his knees. Then, rubbing his wet eyes with the back of his hand he straightened and clung weakly to a timber upright for support.

It was almost midnight when he literally stumbled into Coolidge's office. The marshal was coming through from the locked room that served as Bigfoot's only cell. There was an amused look in his eyes as he watched Warren trip over the step, cling to the back of a chair then sink into it with a barely stifled groan.

'Should have allowed that feller a second shot,' Coolidge said, leaning back against the desk with his arms folded. 'Might have saved me a lot of trouble, you a lot of pain.'

Warren was thinking back. He said, 'I thought I heard a second shot when I was going under. I guess that was you saving my life.'

Coolidge grunted.

'Saving your life, but only by scaring that feller away: I missed with the shot you heard, caught him with the second but it was a wild one in the heat of the moment and he was only winged.'

'That feller was watching me all day. I was warned, but took no heed.'

Coolidge shook his head. 'I spoke to Barney Kay. You both got it wrong. That fellow watching you was just a drifter been here a couple of days. Rode across from the Mex border, I believe – saw him talking to Alex Crow. Here looking for any trouble he could find. He was unlucky, so he left town late in the afternoon.'

'But could have come back.'

'Could have, but didn't. Leastwise, if he did, it wasn't him trying to put a hole in you. The fellow I winged was dark and slim, moved like a shadow.'

'Like a snake,' Warren said, 'striking when least expected.'

Coolidge's eyes narrowed. 'Maybe. As for you preferring the pain, well, experience has taught me pain takes many different forms. Pain from a bullet wound soon passes. Some kinds linger, fester, eat their way into a man's soul and never go away.'

Warren frowned.

'Bit too deep for me. What the hell are you talking about?'

He watched Coolidge push away from the desk, find two glasses and pull a flat bottle of whiskey from a drawer. As he splashed two generous measures into the glasses and pushed one towards Warren, his eyes were speculative.

'There's only two ways of looking at you getting yourself shot. First is that it had nothing to do with what happened to your pa out at the Rocking P. Second is that it did – and that's the one I favour.'

'I agree. Someone's got it in for the Pallisters.'

'Not all of 'em.'

'Nonsense. Whoever he is he tried for Pa and succeeded, tried for me and failed. If you were doing your job, then one of your deputies would be out at the Rocking P now, making sure that gunman doesn't make a try for Rosie.'

'That's not the way I see it.'

'So tell me, how do you see it?'

'You're a smart young feller, why don't you work it out for yourself? This is the second time we've had this discussion, but in case you've forgotten let me repeat what I said the first time: the only ones benefiting from Clayton T. Pallister's death are you and your ma.'

'Dammit, man, he's killed Pa and now he's tried for me. How the hell—?'

Warren broke off. He saw Coolidge nodding slowly

as he watched what he imagined to be the realization of what he had said hit Warren like a hammer blow.

But it was not realization. All Coolidge had done was use questions and insinuations to point Warren in a direction he had already been visualizing when he crossed the street from the doctor's surgery, but balked at taking. Now Warren shook his head. The awful possibility was out in the open, but that in no way made it acceptable.

'If you think my ma, Rosie, is behind the killing of her husband and the attempt on my life,' he said thickly, 'you'd best think again.'

'I've got a better idea,' Coolidge said. 'When you get home, why don't you ask her straight if she hired a gunman to kill Clayton T.?'

Despite the warmth of the evening, a cold shiver racked Warren's muscular frame when he stepped out of the jail. That spasm sent a hot bolt of pain shooting through his wounded shoulder, and with it came the understanding that what had begun with a fatal shooting was leading to complications which would change his life forever.

For a moment he hesitated, teetering on the edge of the plank walk, indecision causing sweat to spring out on his brow.

One way or another, putting that terrible question to his mother was certain to accelerate that change. If she answered in the negative – as he truly believed she would – then relief would be overwhelming, but her trust in him would have gone forever. If she confessed, or lied. . . .

Warren shuddered.

Sucking in a deep breath and deliberately blanking his mind, he stepped off the plank walk. As he took a diagonal path across the street towards the livery barn, movement caught his eye. At the same time he heard the soft murmur of dust-muted hoofbeats and, when he glanced down the street he saw two riders entering town from the west. As he continued across and they drew ever closer, he saw in the uncertain light cast by the oil lamps that they were Mexicans a long way from home – a woman, and a much older man.

And then they were on him.

A fine chiffon scarf was wrapped about the woman's dark hair and the lower half of her face to protect her from the heat and the dust. As she drew level with Warren, she looked down at him. Their eyes met and, for Warren, it was as if an electric shock passed between them. For an instant his step faltered; he almost stumbled. Then the two horses had ridden on by.

Warren had almost reached the far plank walk, his mind in turmoil, when he glanced back down the street. The woman had twisted in the saddle. She was watching him. Even at a distance he thought he saw something in her face, in her eyes; thought perhaps he could see a half-smile curving her lips. Without thinking, he lifted a hand in tentative acknow-ledgement of . . . of what?

He thought he saw her nod as she turned away.

Then he was in the barn, the two riders had pushed on down the street and, fighting to dismiss them and the disturbing incident from his mind, Warren moved to the stall where his horse was stamping impatiently.

FIVE

Close to two o'clock on a warm night, and as Warren Pallister approached the gates to the Rocking P spread he thought he saw, at the distant edge of a stand of trees turned into a dark, shapeless block by the moon's pale light, a rider moving slowly away towards San Miguel Creek. There was no sound, no jingle of harness, no dust kicked up by the horse's hoofs. Briefly, there was a flash of white. Then, even as he watched, the rider disappeared, leaving Warren to blink several times and wonder if what he had seen was nothing more sinister than the movement of branches in the gentle breeze, or the fleeting shape of a prowling coyote made huge by its own shadow.

Then even those thoughts scattered like silent, startled birds as he saw the light in the living-room, his mother sitting at the long table staring fixedly, by the light of a single oil lamp, at the painting of her dead husband.

Warren climbed awkwardly from his horse and

tied it at the rail. The bullet had hit hard as it sliced through the flesh of his left shoulder. It had done little permanent damage, but the wound had stiffened and, with each movement, the dry bandage was pulling at the congealed blood. For a few moments he stood there, debating what to do next. Then, glancing across to the bunkhouse and seeing the faint gleam of an oil lamp through the curtained window, he walked awkwardly across the yard.

Here, too, just a single oil lamp was burning. Al Rickard, still suffering from a high temperature, was a shapeless mound of blankets in his corner bunk. Stocky Jake Furnival was sitting up against the head of his cot with his damaged leg stretched out, and was lazily strumming his guitar. His eyes were closed. Across from him, old Bony Park was listening with obvious enjoyment. He was stretched out on his bunk with his hands behind his head. One stockinged foot was beating time. A smouldering cigarette drooped from his thin lips.

Both men looked towards Warren as he walked in.

'You two are up late.'

'Thinking. They're out there and we're in here, and we're wishing we were out there with them,' Furnival said, placing his guitar flat on his blankets.

'Speak for yourself,' said Bony Park. 'I've done more years on the range than you've spent in hours plucking that contraption – and that's saying something.'

Furnival chuckled, but it was in an absent manner.

He had stretched out on his bunk alongside his guitar, and was studying Warren.

'You hit trouble in town?'

'Came out of nowhere,' Warren said ruefully. 'I was preoccupied when I left the Wild Horses: Brent Coolidge had earlier been giving me a hard time, Alex Crow is sitting on information that could be dynamite, and Barney Kay warned me there was a suspicious character in town showing an unhealthy interest in me.'

'Looks like he was right.'

'Maybe. Someone took a pot shot at me out of the shadows. But according to Coolidge, it wasn't the man watching me who did this.'

He touched his shoulder, deliberately let the talk fall away, inviting comment.

Furnival obliged. 'How could Coolidge be sure?' he said.

'Because he saw the gunman, got off a couple of wild shots. He thinks one of 'em winged the fellow.'

Bony Park stirred, shifted his cigarette, coughed harshly.

'Why don't you get down to the real reason you walked in here, son?'

Warren shook his head. 'There is no real reason—'

'It was Chavez who was here,' Park cut in. 'Like it has been most times of late when your pa was off the spread. The damned Mex rode in, stayed no more than a few minutes talking to your ma, rode out just before you got here.'

44

'I saw him – saw someone.'

'Well now you know.'

Warren nodded slowly, replaying in his mind what he had seen: the shadowy figure at the edge of the trees, the flash of white in the moonlight. . . .

'Mexs of a certain type favour pure white shirts, most of the time,' he observed expressionlessly.

'And bandages, like everyone else,' Furnival said, in a wooden voice, 'when the need arises.'

'Is that what I saw when I was riding in?'

'Only you know what you saw—'

'But what you said suggests—'

'—and if anyone can answer your question, it's the person closest to the Mex, and that was your ma.'

'I'll talk to her,' Warren said, and he swung on his heel and walked out of the bunkhouse.

As he entered the house, he again touched his wound absently, for his mind was already racing ahead to the questions he must ask and to the probable answers.

Rosie Pallister turned as he walked into the room. Her instant, bright smile turned to a look of concern as she saw the white bandages and the way Warren was favouring his left arm as he moved to the table and sat down.

'He almost got you, too, did he?' she said. Her long, greying fair hair was loose. One of her hands toyed with the fine tresses.

Was she nervous, Warren wondered, watching her

45

hands? If so, why? And what was she doing, sitting there at such a time? She was alone in the big room. The window through which the fatal shot had drilled was still without most of its glass. The table was scarred though not broken by the impact of the wagon wheel which had killed her husband. With its broken lamps still hanging forlornly from its rim, the wheel – the closest Clayton T. Pallister had got to a chandelier – now stood against the room's back wall.

What was she waiting for, Warren wondered? Or was the waiting over, he thought bleakly, remembering the figure alongside the dark woods, his talk with Furnival and Park?

'Somebody did,' he said quietly. 'Coolidge saw him try to gun me down as I came out of Barney Kay's, thinks he winged him with a wild shot but couldn't stop him getting away.'

'And you don't know who it was?'

Warren shrugged, then winced and grabbed his shoulder.

'According to Kay, a fellow was watching me for most of the day. The only time I saw him was in the livery-barn. I didn't look twice at him, wouldn't recognize him if I tripped over him. According to Brent Coolidge, that fellow was looking for trouble, but left town when none came his way.'

'But if you see a man carrying a gunshot wound,' Rosie said softly, 'that would be highly suspicious – given what Coolidge claims.'

'Maybe. He shot someone, that's for sure. But

what about you?' He looked hard at her, tried to put meaning into his eyes. 'Any more ideas on who might have shot Pa, and tried to gun me down?'

Rosie frowned. 'Should I have? We were both here, you and I. The shot that killed your father came out of nowhere – out of the blue, so—'

'Ma, what made Pa change seats on the night he died?'

'Why, I did, of course.'

'*You* did?'

'Yes. I was sick and tired of him staring at that damn painting. Most of the time he wasn't listening to a thing anyone said. He'd be stuffing food into his mouth, then he'd look up at that painting and a smug, self-satisfied look would cross his face.'

'And when you asked him to sit somewhere else, he agreed?'

'I told him he could look out of the window for a change, give you a chance to study the painting.'

Knowing how Warren would feel about that, her smile was suddenly mischievous.

'Actually,' she said apologetically, 'I didn't mention you at all. I told him he would be able to look out of the window, talked some nonsense about him being able to keep an eye on the preparation for the round-up – or keep an eye out for that fellow he was always accusing me of getting too close to.'

Warren pursed his lips. 'That would work, on both counts.' He hesitated. 'What about that fellow, Ma? He has been calling frequently, and I know he was

47

here tonight. I've not asked questions before now, but—'

'He's a Mexican, and he works for Meg Murphy and her sister. But you must know that. His name's Raulo Chavez. I believe he's their handyman – no, that's wrong, I'm sure of it.'

'Was he wearing a bandage when you spoke to him tonight?'

Rosie frowned. 'I don't know. Possibly – but I really can't say for sure either way.' She shrugged dismissively. 'Anyway, his only reason for coming here at any time has been to try to persuade me to sell the Rocking P. I told him bluntly there was no chance, not while Clayton T. was alive.'

'I wonder if it is possible, now that he's dead?'

'Now what on earth is that supposed to mean? Are you asking me if I want to sell, if I'm *going* to sell?'

Warren hesitated. 'What I'm wondering is if you are in a *position* to sell.'

'Clarify that one, Warren. I'm getting confused.'

'If, for some reason, you don't inherit – then the ranch won't be yours to keep *or* to sell.'

'I asked you to be clearer, but I still don't know what you're talking about. What do you mean, if I don't inherit? You're not making sense.'

'I'm talking about a complicated and possibly tragic situation,' Warren said. 'A situation as outsiders might perceive it, rightly or wrongly, I don't know. . . .'

His voice trailed off. Rosie had sat back in her

chair. She was watching him closely, yet he knew she was thinking hard. Her eyes narrowed as she concentrated; her fingers tugged absently at her loose hair. Then she nodded slowly, and she half-smiled as her features relaxed.

'Yes,' she said, 'I see what you're getting at now – or part of it. The part I understand clearly is that I'm supposed to have persuaded your pa to change seats so the gunman I'd hired could bring that damn wagon wheel down on his head; I arranged that deliberately to get him out of the way, firstly because the man was a bully, secondly so I could sell the ranch.' She shook her head. 'I'm guessing the tragic bit – as outsiders might *perceive* it – is that I went to all that trouble for nothing. So are you going to tell me what's going on, or do I have to go into town and talk to Alex Crow?'

Warren grimaced.

'I don't know what's going on. Alex Crow sort of does, but he won't say. He mentioned rumours. I don't know where they came from, or what's in them – although I do know the man watching me had talked to Alex, and had ridden into town from the Mex border.' He shook his head. 'But none of that matters. You've admitted you asked Pa to change seats. All I need from you is your word that you did it for the reason you gave me and not—'

'As the last part of a plan to murder your father?' She smiled sadly. 'Do you really need that reassurance from me, Warren?'

He looked at his mother's face, and swallowed. 'No,' he said huskily. 'I've been thinking about this long and hard, on my own for most of the day, with Alex Crow's words tumbling around inside my head. I was confused – but that's no excuse. You're my mother. In my heart I've known all along that you're incapable of cruelty, too sensitive to crush a beetle let alone a full-grown man you've lived with—'

She reached out and touched his hand, silencing him with a glance.

'Enough,' she said softly. 'With your father's passing, the past has given way to the future. I need to ask you now, what you think about the ranch, what you would feel if I decided that it was in our best interests *not* to accept the offers that have been made to me, to turn *down* those offers and—'

And then it was her turn to break off in mid-sentence. Her eyes had flashed towards the window, and now her grip on his hand tightened.

'I heard horses. Someone is coming. I think they're approaching the house.' There was a tremor in her voice. 'It's happening again, isn't it? But at this time, this late – who can it possibly be?'

Her hand flew to her mouth. Her eyes were huge, wide with apprehension. Warren gently lifted her other hand from his. Then he slipped away from the table, drew his gun and flattened himself against the wall alongside the window.

*

From the low rise on the approach to the Rocking P they could look down and across the moonlit yard. They had a clear view of the house, the lamp-lit front room, the man and the woman sitting at the long table.

'She has come this far,' the lean man called Luis Delgado said, 'and still we don't know where she is getting this money.'

'Worse than that,' his companion said, 'we don't know if there is any money available to her, or even if that is the real reason for her being here on the wrong side of the Bravo.' As he spoke, Pepe Herrera, menacing in dark clothing ornamented with glittering conchos and the gleam of several weapons, was wearing a look that was a mixture of mild amusement and smouldering frustration.

'That is true,' Delgado agreed.

He was an older man, the stubble on his face flecked with grey, the hands resting on the saddle horn lean and gnarled. But if anything he was the harder of the two men, and in his dark eyes there was a depth of cruelty that might make casual observers shudder and turn away.

'However,' he continued, eyes that were as black as buttons fixed on the yard and the house's naked front window, 'if there is the smallest chance that what we have heard is even remotely close to the truth, then by riding here we have given *ourselves* a chance.'

'Of becoming rich?' Herrera shrugged

expansively. 'There are other, more certain ways.'

'Which we have tried, and discovered to be uncertain,' Delgado said. 'We have tried many wearisome times over too many years – and look at us. We have tried cattle rustling, we have tried robbery – of both stage coaches and banks.' He grinned at a sudden thought. 'You, Pepe, you have even tried to worm your way into the affections of more than one rich widow.'

'With some success.'

'Hah! A few pesos came your way, scarcely enough to make a bulge in one of your pockets – and so we remain poor. And watched, always, by the Rurales. So now we are in Texas, following a woman who may be here to get her hands on enough money to solve all our problems.'

'Perhaps,' Herrera said, 'she is aware that she is being followed.'

'I think not. At a safe distance we followed her into town. We watched her stop at the jail and go inside. When she came out again, with the town marshal, there was no sign of suspicion. If she had mentioned her fears, he would have looked intently up and down the street, his eyes searching – but he did nothing.'

'He pointed,' Herrera said. 'She followed his directions, and now she is here, and we are here. And if you are right and the money is here also, we know that she will insist that it comes to her in cash, for no poor Mexican would be foolish enough to trust a gringo.'

'And what she takes in cash,' Delgado said, 'can be taken from her.'

Herrera flashed him a look.

'She will fight, tooth and nail.'

'She is a woman. For protection she has with her her father, and he is an old man.'

'You are no chicken yourself,' Herrera said.

Delgado grinned. 'But I am mean, and I am accompanied by a *mal hombre*,' he said. 'Together we will be more than a match for a spitting wildcat and a man whose joints are stiffened with age.'

Then his eyes narrowed.

'You realize,' he said, 'that she has been talking. Because she has spoken of this trip, and the reasons behind it, there are many people in the village who know of her plans. This means that if we we take this vast sum of money—'

'Which may not exist.'

Delgado nodded hurriedly. 'Of course. But if it does, and we take it, then we will not be able to return to Pueblito. She will have a tale to tell, of riches gained then snatched from her, and in her story she will undoubtedly name names.'

'Perhaps,' Herrera said, 'in the taking of the money something will happen that will prevent her from returning to Pueblito; prevent her telling her tale to anyone, anywhere – ever. You see?'

'I see,' Delgado said, again nodding, and in the cruel eyes that had looked on poverty for more than half a century there was a gleam of understanding.

53

'We will see what develops,' he said.

'When the time comes,' Herrera said.

'When the time comes,' Delgado agreed, nodding.

He sat back in the saddle, the old man with the cruel eyes, and as he watched and waited, he took out a slender cheroot and placed it, unlighted, between lips as thin as a knife slash.

SIX

'Are we being too ambitious?'

'That's like asking me if I think we're too old. The answer's always going to be no.'

Meg Murphy, comfortably plump as she reclined in a worn easy chair, smiled at her tall, grey-haired sister. Appearances spoke volumes. Meg had always been the cautious one. Sinéad, her direct opposite, was the sister who took outrageous risks but kept a loaded over-and-under shotgun in case things went badly wrong. *Hidden but handy, she liked to say. That way I know it's there, but to those getting uppity it comes as one almighty shock.*

'Stubbornly saying no doesn't make it the right answer,' Meg said now. 'Besides, the age question brings no consequences other than the possibility of injured pride. Enquiring if it's overly ambitious to lay out Lord knows how many thousand dollars of our savings on a desirable piece of Texas land is pure old-fashioned caution.'

'Add in the buildings and the cattle, and others might put reluctance down to faint-heartedness.'

Again Meg smiled.

'By *others*, you're referring to Raulo, I suppose?'

'Well, he's been rattling on and on about the attractiveness of the Rocking P ever since we took him on as handyman. So insistent has he been that inevitably he's brought me round to his way of thinking, though up to now the idea it might one day be ours has been a pipe dream. But with Clayton T. out of the way—'

'The point I'm raising,' Meg said, her grey eyes serious, 'is do we want, and indeed can we handle, a spread of that size? You're eighty years old, Sinéad, and I'm hanging on to your skirts and drawing ever closer. Add the Rocking P's adjoining acres to our humble homestead where we just about grow enough vegetables to feed ourselves, and what have you got? We'd have a genuine ranch to rival ... I don't know ... Charlie Goodnight's Palo Duro outfit?'

Now it was Sinéad's turn to grin. She was sitting on the edge of her chair close to the flickering log fire which provided the room's only light, her long skirts wrapped about her still slender legs. There was a look of glee on her lined, elfin face, and in the firelight her blue eyes danced.

'Adjoining is exactly right. Rocking P's no more than a couple of miles from here, divided from us only by the San Miguel Creek. Also, it comes complete with cattle and cowboys and wranglers and a cook and a chuck wagon – now, wouldn't that be something?' she said softly.

'Difficult, is what it would be,' Meg said.

'Nonsense. We would sit back and pay others to run it for us.'

'And see the good years' profits wiped out by a single year of drought.'

'Faint heart never won—'

'Fair lady,' Meg finished. 'Wrong proverb, Sinéad.'

'But you must admit it's the right sentiment.'

'I don't know, I really don't. What I do know is we were born back East, we made that long trek from back East, and I've always heard that folks get a hankering to return to their roots to die.'

'If we were about to die, I might agree with you. Me, I have no intention of doing any such thing in the—'

She was interrupted by a discreet knock on the door.

The man who entered at her bidding and stood just outside the circle of light was of medium height, but with an impressive bearing. He was slim of hip, broad of shoulder, and the sheen of his black hair was matched by the steely gleam of the pistol at his belt, the liquid shine in dark eyes that studied each of the women in turn.

'A decision has been reached?' he said, in gentle, accented English.

'Come closer, Raulo,' Meg said. 'Pour three

drinks, and we'll see if we can thrash this out.'

The Mexican crossed to a timber sideboard, poured dark wine into three glasses and carried the women's drinks over to the fire. While they took their first taste he stepped back and waited patiently, the crystal glass held in strong, slender fingers.

'You've hurt yourself,' Meg said.

The Mexican smiled, shrugged, lifted his wrist with its white bandage and shook his head.

'It is nothing. I caught it on a rusty nail. It will pass without trouble. *No hay veneno*: there is no poison.'

'So what's the story they're telling in town, Raulo?' Meg said. 'Are they saying who murdered Clayton T. Pallister?'

'I have not been into town.' He smiled crookedly, the look in his eyes deterring any questions. 'But there are rumours circulating, and from those rumours I would infer that someone had reason to be very angry with Mr Pallister – angry enough to kill him. Someone, perhaps, who was very close to him.'

'What rumours?'

The Mexican shrugged. 'I have heard that one source is the marshal, Brent Coolidge. He has said very little openly—'

'But from what he has said, you've drawn reasonably accurate conclusions?'

'It is not for me to say.'

Meg sighed. 'All right, so what has she been saying? Rosie Pallister? You've been over there talking to her several times in the past few months.

And is it up to her, or does the son, Warren, now have a say?'

'So many questions,' Raulo Chavez said, white teeth flashing beneath his neat moustache as he smiled. 'In answer to the first, she has been saying that, yes, she would sell, but her husband would never agree. Now there is no husband. . . .'

'Right. Murdered by a gunman because someone was angry with him. And you know something, probably the reason for that anger, but you're not going to open up?'

'If I did, I would simply be adding to unfounded rumour; my conclusions could be misguided.' He shrugged. 'As for the son, Warren, it is certain that if a sale were considered then he would be consulted, but. . . .'

'Go on,' Sinéad prompted.

'The estate always goes to the next of kin,' Raulo said. 'As Clayton T.'s wife, Rosie Pallister inherits. It is she who will have the final say, and I am convinced that she wants to sell the Rocking P.'

Now it was Meg who was being drawn in by the possibilities. Her face was flushed, her plump fingers dangerously tight on the wine glass's slender stem.

'You're sure of that? She inherits? And she wants to sell?'

Raulo nodded, then spoke carefully, choosing his words. 'That is what she told me. I have no reason to disbelieve her.'

'All right. That's it then,' Meg said, drawing in a

shaky breath. 'We'll take the buggy into Bigfoot tomorrow morning. We'll talk to the bank, then to Alex Crow.'

'I will drive you myself,' Raulo Chavez said and, as he turned away there was a look in his eyes that went unnoticed by the two women.

It was a look of naked triumph.

SEVEN

The knock on the door was firm.

Warren looked across at Rosie. She was still sitting at the table. Her eyes were flicking nervously between window and door.

Very softly he said, 'Could you make anyone out, see anyone you recognized?'

She shook her head. 'Vague shapes,' she whispered.

Again the knocking – this time louder.

'They must have seen us through the window when they approached the house,' Warren said in his normal voice. 'They know we're here, and if they're openly knocking. . . .'

With his six-gun held down at his side he crossed to the door, put his hand on the knob, then flung it open.

Outside, in the moonlight, a Mexican man took a step backwards. He was tall, very straight. Dark eyes glinted in the weak light of the moon. His hair was grey. His strong hands held a large sombrero flat against his chest.

He smiled, and suddenly to Warren, with his six-gun and his apprehension, the world was a happier place – such was the effect.

'We have come to see the widow, Rosie Pallister,' the Mexican man said.

He removed one hand from his sombrero and gestured to the side, and only then did Warren realize that the man had not come alone.

A woman stepped out of the shadows. She was, Warren saw, the woman he had seen riding into Brownsville. Again, as he turned to face her and his eyes met hers, he experienced a shock that was like an electric charge being administered. His scalp tingled. Incapable of looking away, he saw a smile that he realized was recognition curve her lips, and suddenly his heartbeat quickened.

But this second time, the shock was not overwhelming. As the old man cleared his throat, the spell was broken. Yet release brought no relief. Indeed, as he stood facing the two Mexicans in the waning moonlight and the silence threatened to drag on and become uncomfortable, Warren was hit by a sense of foreboding so strong that he was forced to reach out to the door frame for support.

'All right,' he said at last, fighting to shrug off the feeling of impending doom. 'If you're here to see Rosie, then of course you must come in.'

*

'My name is Maria Pallister,' the Mexican woman said. 'And this is my father, Santiago Garcia.'

'Pallister?' Warren looked at his mother, then returned his puzzled gaze to the Mexican woman. 'What are you saying? That you are a relative of mine, a cousin, perhaps?'

The four were sitting around the big table scarred from what had happened there, the Mexican man and the woman on one long side, Rosie and Warren facing them. On the table there was a pot of hot coffee and four cups. In a sociable manner, but with considerable stiffness, the coffee had been drunk before the talking began.

The Mexican woman's words were almost the first uttered, and they had stunned Rosie and Warren Pallister. Rosie was quick to understand the situation, and recover her poise. For the second time that night she reached out to grasp Warren's hand.

'Do you have proof?' she said to the woman.

'If she's a cousin,' Warren said, 'why are you asking for proof—?'

He stopped his outburst as Rosie lifted a hand.

Maria nodded. 'Yes, of course I have proof. I have the birth certificate, and I have the marriage certificate also.'

'But not the death certificate,' Rosie said, and her hand tightened on Warren's. 'Because of course you are here, as large as life, and so Clayton was. . . ?'

'He was lying,' the woman called Maria said. 'And unfortunately that means that when he walked out of my life, taking with him my son—'

'He was still married to you,' Rosie concluded, 'and has remained so for – what is it, twenty years?'

'Almost twenty-one.'

Warren sat back heavily in his chair. There was an audible thump as the chair's front legs lifted, then fell. Automatically, he reached up to his injured shoulder. His mouth was dry. Once again his pulse was racing.

'I'm . . . I'm dumbfounded,' he said, hearing the catch in his voice. 'This must be the rumour Alex Crow was talking about, but, Goddammit—'

'Warren!'

'I'm sorry.' He glanced apologetically at Maria. 'My mother and I were talking before you came knocking on the door. One of the subjects we were discussing – the possible sale of this ranch – now seems pointless. I had no idea my father had been married twice, but if it's true and you're still alive, then neither of us inherits because my father's marriage to my mother—'

He broke off. His mind, leaping crazily in all directions as he talked, had settled then clung like a limpet to what the Mexican woman had said. Suddenly the startling implications hit home.

'You said he walked out, taking with him your son,' Warren said, and now the catch in his voice had turned to a rasping hoarseness.

Maria Pallister nodded. Her dark eyes were watching him and suddenly, with a frisson of shock that made him bite his lip, Warren realized that they were the eyes he looked at in the mirror every morning when he shaved.

Again Rosie's hand tightened on his, but now her other hand came across and, very gently, she stroked the back of his wrist.

'You're almost a year older than you thought you were,' she said softly. 'You were a baby when Clayton brought you to me—'

'Doesn't matter,' Warren said. He cleared his throat, shook off her hand and pushed back his chair. 'I don't care about any of that,' he said, as he stood up, 'because you've always been my mother and that will never change. What matters is what has been happening, and what happens to us *now*.' He was staring hard at Maria. 'Somebody murdered my father – you must know that, because that's why you're here. But then I was gunned down as I stepped out of the saloon. I'm lucky to be alive, and I'm wondering if you know anything about that; had anything to do with it.'

Maria's smile was sad.

'There is so little you know. I am here legitimately, but there are more important, more powerful people, who are desperate to get a stake here in Texas. They too will use legitimate means, but if those fail – perhaps even if they don't. . . .'

She shrugged, waited.

'What powerful people are you talking about? Who are they?'

'There is a man who owns land in Mexico. His name is Jesus Gonzales. His ranch is measured in square miles. It is situated some distance to the north of Nuevo Laredo, on the Bravo.'

Warren was pacing up and down the table behind his mother. He stopped suddenly, and swung on Maria.

'You're suggesting this man is interested in the Rocking P. But how can that be, how does he know about it?'

'The answer to that lies in your father's frequent absences.'

'Dear God,' Rosie said softly. 'There were several in his last year. Do you mean he was over there in Mexico, playing the big Texan cattleman, tempting the devil?'

'That is what it amounts to,' Maria said. 'But it is now irrelevant. With Clayton out of the way the most stubborn obstacle has been removed.'

'Removed?' Warren said, pouncing on the word. 'Are you saying it was this Gonzales who had him killed?'

'Maybe – but not necessarily. There are others. Word spreads easily in a small village like Pueblito, and we have not been . . . discreet. And so we have realized, perhaps too late, that there are hard poor men as well as powerful rich men.'

'And others closer to our home,' Rosie said, 'who might be short of scruples.'

Warren knew she was talking about the Murphy

66

sisters. He took a deep breath, then leaned forward with his hands braced on the back of his chair.

'Not necessarily,' he said, repeating Maria's words slowly, thoughtfully. Then he shrugged. 'All right. Let's forget responsibility for now and concentrate on facts. Rocking P doesn't belong to us. It *did* belong to Clayton T. Pallister, but with his death it goes to . . . to you.' He shook his head. 'Is that why you're here, to claim your inheritance, sell the Rocking P then return to Mexico with the cash?'

'It is her right,' Santiago Garcia said quietly. It was the first time he had spoken since Warren met him at the front door. His dark eyes were burning, but it was with sincerity, as well as sorrow and understanding for the pain he and his daughter were causing.

'If there is anyone to blame for this mess,' he went on, 'it is Clayton T. Pallister.' His smile was wry. 'But, as is so often the case, the chaos one man creates must in the end be cleared up by others.'

'Yes, and that chaos includes overtures – possibly descending into violence – from a Mexican landowner who will wield the sword should the need arise. Have I got that right?'

'It would seem so,' Garcia said. He thought for a moment. 'Speaking hypothetically, someone placed in such a perilous position would quickly realize that there are two choices: to sell the ranch to the aggressive, powerful landowner, or to sell the property to another interested party, thus passing on the problem.

'The third choice,' Warren said bluntly, 'is not to sell at all.'

Santiago Garcia spread his hands.

'Unfortunately, it is not for us to decide – not for me, not for you, nor for that hypothetical wise man,' he said. 'For, as you have rightly pointed out, the Rocking P has been passed to Maria, and it is now she who must make those tough decisions.'

EIGHT

Maria Pallister and her father, Santiago Garcia, had politely refused Rosie's offer to put them up for the night at the Rocking P. They had already booked a room in Bigfoot's only rooming-house. It was almost two in the morning when they left the Rocking P, a proud man and a remarkably composed woman riding off into the fading moonlight.

There had been no talk left in Rosie or Warren. Emotionally exhausted, they had gone to bed as soon as the drum of hoofbeats had faded into the night.

The next morning, breakfast was a subdued affair, the only sound the rattle of pans and crockery. Rosie had planned to ride into town very early with Warren, and talk to Alex Crow before Maria could get to his office. However, complaining of a headache, she eventually asked Warren to ride into town without her. Warning her to keep the door locked and not to open it for anyone – especially the Murphys' handyman – Warren set out.

Alex Crow was on the plank walk, about to insert the key into his office door when Warren rode into town at a fast canter. Maria and her father were hurrying up the street from the rooming-house. Across the way, a gleaming top-buggy was standing outside the bank. Warren recognized it as belonging to the Murphy sisters; their handyman, Raulo Chavez, was sitting idly in the driving seat with a thin cigar smouldering in one hand and a smug look on his face.

'Alex,' Warren said, pulling in to the hitch rail and hurriedly swinging out of the saddle.

'Been talking to the town council,' the lawyer said, pausing with the key in his hand. 'There's still no sign of cash becoming available for a new windmill.'

'That'll please Mick. One of these days it'll fall down and wreck his livery barn.'

'One of these days,' Crow said, 'the shaft will finally snap; it'll stop working altogether and he'll spend his days walking horses down to the creek for water.'

'Yeah, well.' Warren smiled at the thought. 'We'll cross that bridge when we come to it, but right now you've got a surprise coming your way in the shape of a comely Mexican lady and her pa. I think you've got some points of law to sort out, and you'd best do it before Meg and Sinéad Murphy finish at the bank and get over here.'

'And here's me thinking I had an easy day,' Crow said as the key turned in the lock and the door swung open. 'You'd best come inside – all of you,' he said,

70

as the two Mexicans arrived, breathless and doing their best to appear calm.

But this morning they're not managing it very well, Warren thought, chivalrously stepping aside to let them in. *What they're about to show Alex is explosive, and they're wondering what he and I have been talking about; what, if anything, I've got up my sleeve.*

The office was small and stuffy. Crow banged about raising blinds, opening windows, setting several chairs in a rough half-circle in front of his big desk. As everyone took their places, the plump lawyer sat down in his swivel chair, industriously shifted some papers around on his desk, then settled back and with raised eyebrows looked questioningly at the small gathering.

'It seems,' Warren said, when nobody ventured to speak, 'that Clayton T.'s first wife didn't die after all.' He looked hard at Crow. 'Seems it's no longer a rumour brought into town by a drifter who rode in from the Rio Grande.'

'Ah.' Crow grimaced, then looked directly at Maria. 'Then it's not too difficult to work out who you are, ma'am.'

'I am Maria Pallister,' she said, nodding.

Very quickly, with hands that shook slightly, she took papers from a small purse she was clutching and leaned forward to place then on Crow's desk.

Settling a pair of gold pince-nez on his nose, Crow read them quickly. They were, Warren knew, Maria's birth and marriage certificates. Feeling his heart thumping uncomfortably, he sat and waited.

Eventually, Crow looked up. Again, he looked directly at Maria.

'I can see what they are,' he said to her, 'but what do they prove?'

'They prove I am Maria Pallister, of course, and that I am Clayton T. Pallister's first wife. Only wife,' she corrected, 'because his subsequent marriage to Rosie was illegal.'

'Actually, they don't prove anything,' Alex Crow said. He flicked one of the certificates with his forefinger. 'This one doesn't even prove that you are Maria Garcia. You're carrying these bits of paper, but that's all they are. You could have picked them up anywhere, could be anybody.'

And now Warren felt his heartbeat falter for a different reason. Last night, he and Rosie had questioned the existence of birth- and marriage-certificates, but had not considered the possibility that such papers could be meaningless. But if they were – if Alex Crow had found a hole in Maria's story – then their lives would return to normal: the Rocking P belonged to Rosie; they could keep it, sell it, or simply sit back until they reached a decision.

His hopes were quickly dashed.

'She could be anybody, or nobody,' said the grey-haired Mexican sitting next to Maria, visibly flexing his lean frame in the straight chair. 'However, I am here to tell you that she is who she says she is. The name of the father on those *bits of paper* as you call them is my name. I am Santiago Garcia. I registered the birth, witnessed the marriage, and this woman is my daughter, Maria.'

'Again, I hate to argue the point,' Crow said, 'but you too could be anybody at all unless you have proof—'

He broke off. Garcia was on his feet. He had a paper in his hand. He unfolded it and slammed it on the desk.

'There is your proof,' he said, and he pulled himself erect and looked arrogantly down his nose at Crow.

Crow read the paper several times. Then he sighed. He placed it face down on the desk and looked sympathetically at Warren.

'I can't show it to you. It's an official document, with a passable likeness. An identity document, if you like, but it certainly proves that this man is who he says he is and that he has some standing in the work he does in a certain area of Mexico. And although I must still point out that there is probably another Santiago Garcia out there somewhere—'

There was a short, explosive exclamation of disbelief from Garcia.

'—who could be the man on those certificates, common sense is telling me—'

A second interruption caused him to break off in mid-sentence. There was a sharp rap on the office door. It was pushed open. Meg Murphy walked in. She was followed by her sister, Sinéad. Suddenly Meg, short and bustling, caught sight of the group gathered around the desk. She stopped in the doorway. Her sister, tall and angular, bumped into her – hard. For a moment they stood there, clutching each other as they struggled to regain their balance.

'Goodness,' Meg said at last, catching her breath, 'what on earth is going on here?'

'The possibilities are exciting,' Meg Murphy said musingly, half to her sister, half to herself. 'Clayton T. wouldn't sell the Rocking P, in time Rosie could be persuaded, I imagine – but with the surprise of a new owner from across the border, this could be our lucky day.'

'Unless,' Sinéad said quietly, 'the real Mrs Pallister doesn't want to sell.'

The two ladies from the Murphy homestead were sitting in front of the desk. There was now a shortage of chairs. Warren and Santiago Garcia were standing with their backs to a wall were Alex Crow's framed lawyer's certificates were hanging. Meg and Sinéad had been given a quick run down by Crow on what had emerged in the meeting so far. They had exchanged quick glances when the implications hit home. Their excitement at the revelations was palpable, but they had said very little.

Now, at Sinéad's words, Garcia uttered a soft exclamation.

'Selling is what we must do,' he said. 'I am involved in important work which takes me from my village. My daughter . . . Maria . . . is on her own, and in any case she has no experience of running a ranch, certainly no wish to leave Pueblito, or Mexico.'

Meg Murphy had turned in her chair to listen to him. Her eyes were alight.

'So you *are* willing to sell Rocking P?'

'Whoa there, hold on a minute,' Alex Crow said. 'There's procedures to go through. I won't go into details but they all take time—'

'Pshaw, and phooey as well,' Meg said, cutting him off. 'What we're doing saves time.'

'Possibly. But you're considering buying property from a woman who hasn't yet officially inherited. If this . . . *deal* goes through, the property is then two steps removed from the Pallisters who at present are *still* the rightful owners—'

'Rosie is not a Pallister,' Maria said sharply.

'Which seems to be the crux of the matter,' Meg said. 'You can go through your procedures, Alex, and no doubt will with your usual thoroughness. This way, when it's all over and it's clear Maria is the new and rightful owner, instead of handing deeds to her for her then to pass on to us, you give them straight to Sinéad and me.'

'There is one stipulation which you might find difficult to meet,' Santiago Garcia said, looking hard at the two women.

'You mean if we want to buy, we're going to have stump up the cash?' Meg grinned and patted the fat linen bag she had brought in with her and which now rested in her ample lap. 'We've been to the bank, Mr Garcia. We were hoping to tempt Rosie by waving greenbacks under her nose, but as circumstances have altered—'

'Be careful,' Alex Crow said.

Meg raised an eyebrow.

'What can go wrong, Alex?' she said. 'Make a wild guess if you like, but I'd like your honest opinion about the legal formalities. Can you see *anything* going wrong?'

'If we were back East, or somewhere like Houston, I could see a whole lot going wrong. Most of what we're doing here is probably illegal. Anywhere else, you'd *never* get away with it—'

'But we're not anywhere else, Alex,' Sinéad said sweetly. 'So, come on now, be a good boy and answer Meg's question.'

Crow hesitated. He leaned back in his chair. His fingers were laced across his white shirt front, which was straining against the buttons. He pursed his lips.

Eyes half closed he said, almost as if thinking aloud, 'Clayton Pallister's deceased. There is no will. There is no mortgage on the property, so the deeds are sitting in my safe, not the one over there at the bank. His next of kin is his wife. It seems he was a bigamist, so his only legal wife is sitting here in this room.'

'Indeed she is,' Garcia said quietly. He was watching Crow, and nodding slowly as if urging the lawyer to come to the right decision.

Crow grimaced and ran a hand across his bald head.

'No,' he said. 'Barring another big surprise, when the formalities have been completed, Maria will own the Rocking P.'

'And by then,' Sinéad said, 'she'll have sold it to us.'

'Damn right she will,' Meg said, struggling out of her chair.

'But let me just add this word of caution,' Crow said. 'If things do go wrong, and money has changed hands, there'll be all sorts of complications – made worse because this deal crosses an international border.' He smiled apologetically at Maria; to Meg Murphy he said, 'You will have paid a lot of money for Rocking P. If you find the deal collapses, getting that money back could be very difficult when it's been moved to Mexico and changed into the national currency.'

'Mountains out of molehills,' Sinéad said dismissively.

'Wrong saying again,' Meg said, grinning, 'but it'll do. Maria, the quicker we agree a price, the quicker you can get back to Mexico. Come on, let's go somewhere and talk.'

NINE

Meg Murphy decided that the logical place for her and Sinéad to talk privately to Maria Pallister was out at the homestead. She put this to Maria and her father. They agreed, but said that first they had several things to do. Meg thought this unusual, almost strange in the circumstances, but she acquiesced. The four arranged to meet again at midday, when Maria and her father would follow the Murphys' top-buggy out to the homestead.

The excuse Maria and her father had made was only partly true.

Meg and Sinéad stayed behind, chatting to Alex Crow. A short while later they left for the dry goods emporium and Crow walked down the street to talk to the marshal, Brent Coolidge. Warren Pallister crossed the street to the saloon. Santiago Garcia took his daughter's arm, and together they walked down the street to the café, where he ordered breakfast.

When that was finished, and they were drinking

their second cup of coffee, he broached the subject that had made them walk away from the Murphys.

It was Maria who had spotted possible danger.

Now, Santiago Garcia said, 'Are you absolutely certain?'

'He works for Jesus Gonzales,' Maria said. 'I have already told Rosie to be very careful, because Gonzales has his eyes on the Rocking P. And now I have recognized this man, across the street in the top-buggy.'

Santiago sipped his coffee, then frowned.

'But why is this man—?'

'Raulo Chavez.'

'Yes, Chavez.' Garcia nodded, committing the name to memory. 'Does this Chavez know you?'

She shook her head. 'No. I saw him once or twice, in Pueblito, and he was pointed out to me as a bad man. But Chavez did not see me.'

'So, if Gonzales wants the Rocking P, why is this man Chavez working as a handyman for the Murphys?'

'There is a gringo saying,' Maria said. 'There is more than one way of skinning a cat. One of the girls from Pueblito is a maid at the Gonzales place. Clayton T. was frequently a guest there. Gonzales used his powers of persuasion, but Clayton always stubbornly refused to sell. I think Gonzales grew tired of waiting, and used Chavez to remove him.'

'Again, my question: so why is Chavez with the Murphys?'

'Because Gonzales is a cunning man. Somehow he learned that Meg Murphy and her sister were interested in buying the Rocking P. He knew that they also would be obstructed by Clayton. Gonzales eased their way by getting Chavez to kill him—'

'But with Clayton T. out of the way,' Garcia interrupted, 'then surely Gonzales could buy the Rocking P for himself.'

'Gonzales was convinced, from his talks with Pallister, that the Rocking P would never be sold to a Mexican landowner. He assumed that even with Clayton T. gone, Rosie – and perhaps the authorities – would have those same sentiments and no sale would go ahead. Who knows, perhaps there may be genuine legal obstacles. However, if the ranch goes to the Murphys, it will be in the hands of two vulnerable women. Gonzales will move in, threaten them. In the end he will get the Rocking P, and if the threats are severe enough it will fall into his hands very cheaply.'

'So where is the danger? It is not our concern. Gonzales knows nothing about your claim to the Rocking P.'

Maria shook her head.

'Then when this Gonzales becomes involved with the Murphys, we will already have made the sale to them and be on our way back to Mexico.'

Maria's only answer was a direct stare that dared him to look deeper.

Santiago Garcia stared down at his empty

breakfast plate, absently turned it round and round with his finger. He knew the answer to his own question. Trouble was, that presented them with a dilemma. He looked up at her. She was still watching him.

'So what do we do?' Garcia said thoughtfully.

'We sell, as planned.'

'Even though then, if your reasoning is correct, we will be guilty of putting those two old women into great danger?'

'Yes, even then, because we can walk away with clear consciences,' Maria said. 'How we do that is by going now to the town marshal, Brent Coolidge, and telling him what we know. The problem is then in his hands.'

Santiago smiled, and reached across to touch her face gently with the back of his fingers.

'You always were so clever,' he said softly.

'There is another thing,' she said. 'And this other thing means that we too could be in danger.'

'Go on.'

'I have seen this Chavez, and I know he is involved with Gonzales. But I have also seen two men from our village. They are called Delgado and Herrera.'

'Ah, yes,' her father said softly. 'They are *alborotadores*, troublemakers. If they are here, they have followed us. If they have done that, it can be for but one reason.' He spread his hands. 'So again, I ask you, what do we do?'

'For now, nothing. But when we have the money in

our possession and we must make that long journey back to the Bravo, then we seek help.'

'From?'

'Warren Pallister.' She pursed her lips, her eyes gleaming. 'He has found his true mother. He will not want to lose me again. If all we need is an escort, and it will give him almost a week with me. . . .'

Garcia nodded slowly, a faint smile of approval at his daughter's cunning tugging at his lips. Then he pushed away the plate he had been toying with, and together they left the café and crossed the street. Ten minutes later, after a brief conversation with Marshal Brent Coolidge at the jail, they located Meg and Sinéad Murphy, told the sisters they had finished their business sooner than expected and were ready to proceed to the Murphy homestead.

They rode out of Bigfoot in the heat of the morning, following the top-buggy driven by the man called Raulo Chavez.

Outside the saloon, Luis Delgado and Pepe Herrera watched them go. They were sitting on the plank walk with their backs to the wall, their sombreros tipped forward so that their dark and watchful eyes were shaded, their unshaven faces in deep shadow. From that position they could watch the world go by and, as they had been there since early morning, very little had escaped their notice.

They had watched the four people enter the lawyer's office. Garcia and his daughter, they knew;

the lawyer's name was on his brass shingle; they also recognized the fourth man, from their ride out to the Rocking P – Warren Pallister. A short while later, two women who appeared to be in their seventies or eighties had emerged from the bank, spoken briefly to Raulo Chavez – again a person known to them. Then those women had somewhat unsteadily crossed the street, and they too had gone into the lawyer's office.

Casually, Delgado had climbed to his feet and strolled down the plank walk. Alongside the top-buggy where Raulo Chavez was engaged in conversation with a clerk who had stepped out of the bank for a break from work, Delgado paused to apply a match to his cigar. His back to the top-buggy, he listened for a few moments then, trailing blue smoke, he returned to his companion.

'Two sisters,' he had said, flopping down against the wall without looking at Herrera. 'The Murphys. They've just withdrawn a heap of cash.'

Herrera had thought in silence for a few moments. Then he had frowned.

'Pallister is in there, in the lawyer's office, and there is a lot of cash. If this is to do with the sale of Rocking P to the Garcia woman, where do those older women fit in?'

'It is confirmation, the rumours have become truth,' Delgado had answered. 'Maria Garcia, the young woman from Pueblito, owns the Rocking P; it has fallen into her hands. And now she is about to sell it to those women, the Murphys.'

'We don't know for sure.'

'So we follow them,' Delgado says. 'Then, when we see that the Garcia woman and her father have struck a deal, and have the money, we will know for a fact that very soon we will be rich men.'

'There is no need to follow them,' Herrera said. 'If a deal is struck and the money changes hands, the Garcias will return this way.'

'We cannot be sure of that. The Rocking P is to the south, on the San Miguel Creek. What if those sisters also have a place in that direction? When a deal is struck, why will Garcia and his daughter not make directly for Laredo – which is in a south-westerly direction?'

'Because they have been sleeping in the rooming-house, and their belongs remain there. When the deal is closed, they are forced to return to Bigfoot.'

'Also,' Delgado said, nodding agreement, 'it is possible that the deal will need to be closed in front of the lawyer – who is the most likely person to hold the deeds which will be handed over to those two sisters. Yes,' he said, a thin smile creasing his old, scarred face, 'they will come back this way, and we will be ready.'

And so, later, when the top-buggy left town closely followed by Garcia and his daughter, Delgado and Herrera had remained where they were, tipped their sombreros a little further forward over their faces and prepared with quiet confidence for a long wait.

One hour later, Brent Coolidge stepped out of his office and stretched his stiff joints. The sun was hot. It felt pleasant on his ageing frame. As he stood and rolled a smoke, George Gelert strolled down from the saloon. The two men stood in silence, Gelert leaning with his back against the warm wall of the jail, Coolidge closer to the edge of the plank walk surveying what he always liked to think of as his town.

Both men turned at the clatter of hoofbeats.

'Mexicans,' Gelert said without moving. 'Three of 'em. That makes five new arrivals in a couple of days. Chavez has been here a while – and we're a hundred miles from the Rio Grande. What the hell's going on?'

Coolidge didn't answer. His eyes were narrowed against the sun and the smoke from his cigarette. He'd listened to Alex Crow when the lawyer had strolled down from his office. A little while later he'd had a visit from the old Mexican and his daughter who had stood with dignity as they told a preposterous tale. Now he watched the three riders head up the wide main street, and within him a worm of uneasiness stirred.

The Mexican on the lead horse was an imposing figure. He was dressed in fine clothes. His bearing was upright, and as his eyes swept the street from beneath the shade of his broad sombrero, his gaze was imperious.

The men behind him, on the other hand, were from the dregs of humanity – in Coolidge's opinion. Bandits, he reckoned, and in his time, in his younger days, he had come across a few of their kind.

So what did it mean? Two Mexicans, an old man and a young woman, had ridden into Bigfoot, booked rooms at the rooming-house, then ridden out to the Rocking P. Now, a day later, three more greasers were in town. Coincidence was a word missing from Coolidge's vocabulary. So there had to be a connection.

'If it was that Raulo Chavez killed Clayton T.,' Gelert said, his musing breaking into Coolidge's thoughts, 'then this here flood of Mexicans must be connected to him, the Murphys and ultimately to the Rocking P.'

'Which is exactly what that girl Maria and her father just warned me about,' Coolidge said, swinging away from the street as the Mexicans rode on by. 'I reckon it's high time I had a long talk to Rosie Pallister.'

TEN

Warren left the saloon after a long, cool drink and a short chat with Barney Kay. The saloonist had been able to watch most of the comings and goings across the street without moving from behind his bar. After listening to Warren's account of what had been discussed at the Rocking P and in Alex Crow's office, it was he who had seen the three Mexicans ride up Bigfoot's wide thoroughfare. He pointed them out to Warren. Warren glanced towards the sun-drenched street, caught a brief glimpse of the caballero and his two sinister cohorts, and decided there and then that things were hotting up. The haughty son-of-a-gun at the head of the trio was surely the landowner, Jesus Gonzales. It was time to return to the Rocking P and Rosie. If there was trouble brewing, a couple of crocks and an old wrangler left out of the fall round-up would be no match for two ruthless Mexican bandits.

Yet it was not until Warren was nearing the

Rocking P that he realized his first taste of trouble was coming from another direction. Aware of a rider closing in on him, he resolutely kept his head to the front. It was only when he was out of the saddle and tying up in front of the house that he turned to face Brent Coolidge.

Coolidge was tumbling from the saddle like a man feeling age in his bones. He grimaced as he straightened out the kinks. But the intimidating onset of infirmity had not dulled his mind, and his eyes were sharp as he swiftly surveyed the immediate vicinity.

'Those three greasers rode out of town,' he said, 'but I guess they weren't heading for Rocking P. Would I be wrong in thinking they'll be over at the Murphys joining up with that fancy man who's been visiting your ma?'

'What makes you think I'd know the answer?'

'Because when you crossed the street to the Wild Horses, Alex Crow strolled down to the jail and brought me up to date with what he knows. He's done that a couple of times. Like a can of worms being opened is how he's describing what's developing. Part of it's to do with a Mexican called Gonzales working all kinds of trickery to get his hands on Texas land. That was later confirmed by that girl Maria and her pa.'

'If you've been told that much, you must know that it no longer has anything to do with me or Rosie.'

88

'Because you don't own Rocking P? That it passed from Clayton T. to his one and only wife who's come back from the dead? Sure, that too. Trouble is, before last night at the earliest, your ma didn't know that, did she?'

Warren was walking ahead of them towards the house. He saw Rosie standing in the big room, looking tense. When he reached the front door he turned to confront the man who was close on his heels.

'So why have you ridden all this way?'

'You already know why. The only surprise you should feel is that it's taken so long in coming. Like I said in town, your ma's got some explaining to do. And part of it could have something to do with that bullet wound you're nursing.'

Warren's lips tightened. He walked straight into the house and the big living room without extending an invitation to Coolidge. Rosie was still standing, waiting. Warren jerked his head meaningfully as the marshal followed him in. Her eyes widened. When she sat down at the table it was heavily, and her face was pale.

'I won't beat about the bush,' Coolidge said, hat in hand. 'It's a straightforward question I have to ask you, Mrs Pallister—'

'Apparently that's not my name. Not any more – or, indeed, it seems it never was.'

The old marshal winced. 'Legally, it still is, in my eyes. And I find it difficult to change my ways. But that's not the point. The other night, before he got shot, Clayton T. changed seats at this table. You asked him to. Now, did you do that at the bidding of that fellow Raulo Chavez?'

'I don't want to answer that,' Rosie said.

'Ma. . . .' Warren said, warningly.

She held up her hand.

'It's all right. I've done nothing wrong. Raulo's a nice man. In between discussing Meg and her sister buying the Rocking P—'

'Which I'm sure they've now done,' Warren said. 'The meeting with Alex went as expected. The last time I saw Meg and Sinéad Murphy, they were in their top-buggy being followed home by Maria and her father.'

Rosie's smile was sad. 'All right, so what's done is done. I'm sure Raulo's advice was good, and I . . . I'm not ashamed to say that, with Raulo, I enjoyed some unusually pleasant conversations.'

'Don't you think that sounds a little weak?' Coolidge said.

Rosie lifted a stubborn chin.

'It might do. But you have no understanding of the man I always believed to be my husband. Conversation was not his strong point, especially when I was involved—'

'I mean weak in a different way,' Coolidge said. 'I'm suggesting what you enjoyed with Chavez amounted to much more than cosy chat.'

'Like what?' Warren said. 'And is this coming from

guesswork, or from something you've heard?'

For a few moments, Coolidge stood without speaking. Rosie indicated a chair. He smiled his thanks, and sat down. Warren drifted away and stood with his hips resting against the sideboard.

After a few moments, the marshal sighed.

'Not guesswork, exactly,' he said, in response to Warren's question. 'Could call it inspired reasoning, I suppose – though only Mrs Pallister can be the judge of that.'

'Get on with it,' Warren said softly. He swung round, splashed drink into a glass, pointedly neglected to offer one to Coolidge.

'See,' Coolidge said, 'I understood your husband only too well, Mrs Pallister—'

'For God's sake, Brent, you know my name, don't you?' Rosie said, irritably.

Coolidge dipped his head. 'OK, Rosie – and, as I was saying, understanding Clayton T. the way I did I know that he was a big-headed son-of-a-bitch – if you'll pardon my language – and kind of slow-witted. I reckon either you or Chavez, or the both of you together, could easily have dreamed up some pretext to get him away from the head of the table and under that wagon wheel—'

'He wouldn't do it, without damn good reason,' Warren said bluntly.

'But he did,' Coolidge said. 'And your ma's already told you it was at her bidding.'

'Oh, come on—'

91

'And if it was,' Coolidge pressed on, 'then it seems to me your ma's at the very least an accessory to murder, at worst as guilty as hell alongside the man who pulled the trigger.'

'Then talk to him,' Warren said, slamming his glass down. 'Pull Chavez in, put the right questions to him.'

'Oh, I will,' Coolidge said. 'But my question now is, was he acting alone, or did Rosie know exactly what was going to happen if she got Clayton to change seats? And without an answer to that question, what do I do with your ma while I'm waiting to talk to Chavez?' He shifted his gaze, and his face softened. 'What do I do with you, Rosie?'

'Nothing,' she said flatly. 'I'm not going anywhere—'

She broke off. Her eyes flashed to Warren, her face stricken.

'See what I mean?' Brent Coolidge said softly. 'You're on land you don't own, in a house that's not yours. Right now, at the speed things are progressing, I can't even be certain where you'll be this time tomorrow – and when I'm investigating a serious crime, uncertainty is something I cannot allow.'

ELEVEN

It was a short while after noon.

Meg Murphy's chubby face was glistening with perspiration. Her cheeks were flushed. She was looking across at her sister with eyes bright with excitement. But there was an element of restrained panic in there too; the look one might see on the upturned face of someone who's jumped without a lot of thought into murky waters, and discovered they're too deep and inhabited by monsters.

'Broke,' Meg said, shivering deliciously.

'But property rich,' Sinéad said.

'Not much good if we've no working capital, no cash for the day-to-day bills.'

'Should've thought of that. We didn't, so now we've got to deal with it.'

'By borrowing? This morning we were well off. It's afternoon, less than ten minutes ago we finished buying a ranch from Maria Pallister and suddenly we're staring debt in the face.'

'Grief often treads upon the heels of pleasure,' Sinéad said.

'Mm. You always did get your quotations wrong. That's to do with getting wed – the next bit's *marry in haste, repent at leisure* – but I suppose it fits; it was nice while it lasted, wasn't it?'

'And it's not over, sweetie,' Sinéad said, softly, encouragingly, as Meg turned her face away, on the brink of tears.

Suddenly the inner door banged open. Startled, both ladies turned to face it as saturnine Raulo Chavez came through from the rear of the property. Almost in the same instant the fierce clatter of hoofs from directly in front of their small house jerked their gaze towards the window.

Standing with his back to the door, Chavez said, 'It seems that suddenly you are very popular,' and it was Meg who noticed at once that all trace of gentleness had left the Mexican's voice and manner. 'News travels fast,' Chavez said, 'or perhaps it is that for some time this news has been eagerly awaited.'

'Or worked for, then communicated by a sneaky devil with a well-oiled tongue,' Sinéad said bluntly. 'No names mentioned because my meaning's clear: what the hell's going on, Raulo?'

Before the Mexican could answer, a violent kick sent the front door bursting open. Bright sunlight flooded in as it crashed back against the wall. A Mexican in dusty clothing half fell into the room, thrown forward by momentum. He grabbed the door for support with a hand like a claw, and leered at Meg and Sinéad. A second Mexican stepped swiftly through the opening, pistol in hand. He had a scarred face, and the pale-yellow eyes of a bird of prey. He cocked the pistol noisily, and took a pace to the side.

Then, like royalty stepping on to a red carpet, a third man haughtily entered the room. A cruel smile twisted his thin lips. His attire would not have looked wrong on a matador; his poise would have graced any bullring. He was carrying a black leather Gladstone bag. Sinéad had him pegged as a gentleman landowner, a *caballero*, and she looked with understanding at the cold, dark eyes and noticed with surprise that no gun-belt encircled the man's slim hips: he was unarmed.

Leaves the violence to his henchmen, she thought with trepidation.

'Don't look now,' she said bleakly, 'but I think we're about to get down to the real business of the day.'

She came up out of her chair, smoothing her long, faded gingham frock with steady hands. She thrust out her arm to restrain Meg, who was struggling to rise, then looked grimly at the well-dressed Mexican.

'I never did believe in coincidences. The day we acquire a parcel of rich Texas land a dandy from across the border waltzes into our humble dwelling, licking his lips. Within the hour. Carrying a leather bag – d'you see that, Meg? Can't you hear those pesos jingling?' Sinéad grinned mockingly. 'Got a name, have you, Mr *Gentilhombre*?'

'*Por cierto*. I am Jesus Gonzales.'

'There you are, you see, that says it all: he's Gonzales,' Meg said, brushing aside Sinéad's restraining arm and gaining her feet. 'Anyway, whoever Gonzales is he's come all the way from Mexico just to see us, and I think you're being very rude.'

'The manner of his entry raised my hackles.'

'That wasn't him, that was his underlings, his *subordinados*,' Meg said, rolling the Spanish word, 'and he can't be entirely responsible for their bad behaviour.'

'But I am responsible,' Gonzales said, 'and I beg your forgiveness. The man with the restless hands is Rubio; considering his unusual eyes, Blanco could not have wished for a more suitable name.' Gonzales shrugged. 'They speak very little English, so you will find that they are men of few words. And, perhaps an unfortunate trait to be found in two such powerful men, their exuberance overpowers their sense of propriety. They endeavour to protect me with an intimidating presence when, as I am here only to complete a simple business deal with two elegant ladies, it is clear I have no need of protection.'

'Indeed you don't, you flatterer,' Meg said, and flashed a quick look at Sinéad. 'So, you old smoothy, what's this simple deal?'

'Why,' Gonzales said, 'I have learned from Raulo

that you have acquired a ranch you do not need. I am a generous man. It will be financially difficult for me, but I am willing to take this encumbering property off your hands.'

'Then you're in for a hell of a shock, Gonzales,' Meg said bluntly. 'Sinéad, why don't you slip out back and fix these men a fortifying drink?'

As Sinéad left the room, Gonzales flicked a hand at the man called Blanco. He nodded, spun his pistol into its holster. Then he strode across the room in pursuit of her.

It looked as if Meg, still standing by her chair, tried to get out of his way. She turned awkwardly. As she twisted, fighting for balance, her feet became entangled in a loose rug. She gave a little squeal, and fell sideways. She flung out both hands. One hooked in Blanco's shirt front. Buttons popped as it ripped open. Her other hand caught his gun-belt. She hung on, fell heavily against his thighs. Meg's considerable weight pulled him down. His leg collapsed beneath him. He finished up on one knee, leaning sideways with his left hand flat on the floor.

Casually, as if attempting to get up, Meg used her weight to push him all the way down. In the same movement, still on her knees, she whipped his pistol out of his holster, held it in both hands and drew back the hammer. Then, replacing clumsiness with the agility of a cat, she sprang to her feet.

Sinéad Murphy stepped out of the kitchen. At her slender waist she held an over-and-under shotgun. It was comfortably cradled, lazily covering the four men. Her forefinger was crooked around the trigger.

A tense, uneasy silence settled over the room. Outside in the sunlit yard a twig snapped with a sound like a pistol shot. Rubio actually started. He made as if to turn towards the window, then remembered the two guns pointing in his general direction and became still.

'Your move, Gonzales,' Sinéad said. 'You were about to tell us all about taking an encumbering ranch off our hands.'

Gonzales released his breath explosively. He was still holding the Gladstone bag. He lifted his free hand, palm out placatingly, and shook his head slowly.

'It is a simple financial transaction,' he said. 'I am prepared to pay you a sum of money, in cash. But now I am offended, because I do not understand this need for guns.'

'And we don't understand this need for gun*men,*' Meg Murphy said. 'One of your faithful *subordinados* used his boot to kick our door in. Both of them look as if their main trade is armed robbery. Their presence here makes us suspicious, as does the fact that you cunningly planted a man here weeks ago and he's been busily sowing seeds.'

Gonzales's eyes widened ingenuously. He glanced across at Raulo, who had positioned himself against one of the side walls well away from the sunlight flooding in through the front window.

'But that was merely the natural caution of an

experienced businessman,' Gonzales said. 'I needed to be sure of the . . . integrity . . . of the people I would be dealing with—'

'Pull the other one,' Sinéad said shortly. 'Or, better still, spell out your offer. This shotgun's getting heavy. My hands are squeezing ever tighter, and for you that could be very dangerous.'

'Then, if you will permit me,' Gonzales said, 'I have here a prepared bill of sale, in duplicate, so that it can be signed by both parties. . . .'

He placed the Gladstone bag on the table and snapped it open. From it he took two folded sheets of paper. He extended them towards Sinéad. She shook her head and used the shotgun's gleaming barrels to gesture towards Meg.

Somehow managing to keep the six-gun levelled, Meg used her free hand to take the papers from Gonzales. She opened them with a flick of the wrist and quickly skimmed through them. Then, smiling crookedly, she held them up so that her sister could grasp the essenfial details.

Sinéad's eyes registered disgust.

'You're offering way below what we just paid for the Rocking P,' she told Gonzales.

His smile was sympathetic. 'If that is true, then you paid over the odds.'

'Accepting a pittance for it now would compound the foolishness. Or, looked at from your position, it would be tantamount to that armed robbery Meg mentioned.'

'And now you insult me, as well as my men,' Gonzales said stiffly. He took several steps backwards, shaking his head. 'Blanco and Rubio are honest men who cannot be blamed for their sinister looks' – he used a sweeping gesture as if bringing two timid sheep into the comfort of the fold – 'and to call my offer robbery of any kind, armed or otherwise—'

The drone of his voice, his movement out of the circle and his ploy of drawing attention to Rubio and Blanco, had the desired effect. Both Meg and Sinéad automatically looked at the two Mexican gunmen as Gonzales flapped his arm. That misdirection was their undoing.

There was a soft whisper of sound as, in the comparative shadow up against the side wall, Raulo drew his six-gun. There was the louder click as he cocked the weapon. Instantly, Sinéad swung the shotgun towards him, and pulled the trigger.

There was an intense flash, a tremendous roar. The gleaming barrels bucked. The recoil drove the butt into Sinéad's shoulder. At close range, the powerful charge of lead removed Raulo's face. What was left of the lean Mexican was driven backwards. Blood, flesh and fragments of bone flew in a fine, pink cloud. Then his body slammed against the wall.

But in that small room the shotgun blast had been shattering. The Murphys were two ladies of considerable age. The roar and the muzzle-flash assailed ears and eyes, leaving behind a shrill ringing and disorientating crimson after-images. The detonation, and the terrible destruction it had wreaked, left Meg and Sinéad dazed and shaken. Stunned, they were painfully slow to recover.

And Rubio and Blanco were already in motion before the dead Raulo hit the floor. To add to the confusion, they charged at the two sisters at different times, and from different directions. The Murphys stood no chance.

Rubio leaped across the room and pounced on Sinéad. His ugly hands clamped on the shotgun. She tried to pull back, aware of his immense strength, the reek of stale sweat and bad breath. With a vicious twist he wrenched the weapon from the tall old lady's hands. As he turned, holding the shotgun high, his left elbow continued around and slammed into Sinéad's jaw. She went down slackly, eyes rolling.

Blanco deliberately delayed his attack for the time it took Rubio to grab the shotgun and knock Sinéad senseless. Then, as Meg stared at her sister in horror, he stepped forward. With a wide sweep of his booted foot, he kicked her legs from under her. She shrieked and went down sideways, her left arm doubled beneath her. There was a sickening crack as her wrist snapped. The six-gun flew from her right hand. Already moving away from Sinéad, Rubio caught it deftly in one of his clawed hands. He grinned at Blanco as Meg sank back, moaning.

The bills of sale, held by Meg but dropped in the few seconds of explosive action, fluttered to the floor.

'So in the end, despite my efforts, the outcome was

determined by violence,' Gonzales said. 'Nevertheless, I am a businessman of honour; I am determined that the simple deal I had envisaged will proceed and be completed as planned.'

Stepping forward imperiously, he held out the Gladstone bag with its jingling contents and dropped it heavily on to the bills of sale.

'Those papers will be signed, and countersigned, when the ladies wake up.' He smiled thinly. 'I am an impatient man, and I have waited long enough. Blanco, fetch a pitcher of cold water from the kitchen so that their return to consciousness will be swift.'

TWELVE

Maria and her father, Santiago Garcia, had almost been caught cold by the thunderous approach of the Mexican riders. They had walked out of the Murphys' house with Maria clutching the fat linen bag Meg had carried from the bank to Alex Crow's office and then home in the top-buggy, climbed on to their ponies, then exchanged startled glances when they realized the swelling pound of horses' hoofs meant unknown riders were rapidly approaching the Murphys' homestead.

At Garcia's snapped command they had ridden the thirty yards or so that carried them to the edge of thick woods, then quickly slipped from their saddles and led their mounts deep into the crackling, crunching shadows beneath the thick canopy of leaves.

From there, Garcia's arm holding his daughter's trembling body close to him, they had watched the three riders burst from the trail into bright sunlight, tumble from their horses and approach the house. Maria had gasped as one of the men kicked open the door. They had watched the two men Garcia at once dismissively described as *rufianes* enter the house one after the other, to be followed at once by a third man of imposing appearance and noble bearing.

'Jesus Gonzales,' Maria had said, a quiver in her voice. 'It is as I explained to you when we were in the café. Gonzales is determined to get his hands on the Rocking P. We have sold it to the Murphys – and now, here he is with those . . . those *bastardos.*'

From that moment they had listened in silence. They had heard nothing, seen nothing but the occasional vague shape moving against the window. Even Maria, whose eyes and ears were sharper than her father's, had made no sense from the glimpsed movements and detected only the occasional raised voice. Then, suddenly, what to them had always been an ominous silence was split by the roar of a powerful gun. It had been immediately followed by a series of bangs and thuds, then a woman's shriek of terror.

At that sudden outbreak of unseen violence – itself followed by yet more ominous quiet – Maria had closed her eyes and buried her head in her father's chest. Now, he gently pushed her away from him.

'We can only guess what has happened inside that house,' he said softly. 'But it is obvious that a climax of some kind has been reached, and so sooner or later those men will leave again. When they do, we must be far away from here.'

Maria nodded. Her face was a pale blur in the darkness.

'I have explained that also, with regard to the two men from Pueblito,' she said. 'But now more than ever we need an escort on our ride to the Bravo. The Rocking P—'

'Which we have just sold to the Murphys, and which has now almost certainly been forcibly taken from them by this man Gonzales—'

'—is a few miles away across San Miguel Creek. If we ride there now, and Warren is agreeable, we can be on our way to the Bravo and the border before dusk, put many miles behind us during the night.'

'You are right, and your ideas are sound. However, to get even as far as the Rocking P we must proceed with extreme caution,' Garcia said. 'This yard, between here and the house, is too open, and the window is too convenient for those men inside.

'But we cannot wait here until dark—'

'Come,' he said softly, 'we will start now, but lead the horses through the woods. The extra time that will take will be worth it if we make it safely across the San Miguel.'

When Maria and her father rode in, Warren Pallister and Bony Park were on their knees in the dust of the Rocking P's corral, examining a pinto with a bad case of cinch-sores. Leaving Park with instructions to salve the horse's infected areas – at which the old wrangler spat contemptuously because he'd already worked that out for himself – Warren walked across the yard to meet the riders.

The two Mexicans were, he noticed, looking decidedly trail-worn and frazzled. As they dismounted, Maria glanced nervously over her shoulder, looking back the way they had come. She was clutching a linen bag Warren recognized. When she heard his approach she turned quickly towards him. Her relief was obvious: the tension drained from her shoulders, and her face lit up.

'I was so worried,' she said enigmatically, and Warren frowned.

'You'd better come inside, both of you,' he said. 'You can have a cool drink while you tell me what's been going on.'

He left them in the big living room, found a pitcher of lemonade and glasses in the kitchen, and carried drinks through on a tin tray. They accepted them gratefully. As he sat opposite them at the scarred table and they quenched their thirst, he studied them more closely.

Clearly they had been riding hard. From the snags in their clothing he guessed they had forced their way through scrub. Their pants were still damp to the knee: they had forded the San Miguel so must have come, directly or indirectly, from the Murphy sisters' homestead.

Maria was watching him.

'Where is Rosie?' she said softly.

'She's ridden into town with Brent Coolidge.'

'The marshal? So this has something to do with your father's murder?'

'I believe that's what they'll be discussing.'

'But she has not yet been arrested?'

Warren hesitated. 'I don't know about that yet, or even if she ever will be arrested.' Then he shook his head impatiently. 'But I didn't invite you in to talk about Rosie. You said you were worried. Why was that?'

'I was worried that you might not be here, my son,' Maria said, and as she met his gaze, her eyes were limpid pools of emotion.

'Why would that have bothered you?'

'She has a favour to ask of you,' Santiago Garcia said, breaking his silence. 'However, before she proceeds, it is better if I bring you up to date with events. There have been certain unusual developments. Added to what we had already witnessed in Bigfoot, we believe your mother is now in considerable danger.'

First *my son* from Maria, now *your mother* from Garcia, Warren reflected. A deliberate assault on his feelings, the calculated use of evocative words? She was about to ask him a favour. Either he was right in believing they were making his refusal ever more difficult, or he was being cruelly cynical, seeing cunning where there was genuine compassion.

Mildly amused, he listened as Garcia began to describe what had happened since he and his daughter had followed the Murphys' top-buggy out

107

of Bigfoot. His amusement turned to understandable yet irrational resentment when he learned Maria had sold the Rocking P to the Murphy sisters, then to shocked disbelief when Garcia told of the eruption of violence they had heard while hiding in the woods.

'And you didn't remain there long enough to see the outcome?'

Garcia grimaced. 'If we had remained, it is possible that man Gonzales would have learned of our presence.'

'Perhaps, but if you had stayed hidden until they left, you might have been able to help those poor women.'

'It was a difficult decision,' Garcia said, spreading his hands.

'Not swayed in any way, of course, by all the money you're carrying in that linen bag.' Warren shook his head reproachfully, then turned to Maria. 'Well, you made that decision, you must live with it, and now I suppose you're heading home. So, what do you want from me?'

'I am worried, *we* are worried,' Maria said. 'Not about Gonzales; he is a rich man, and he is unscrupulous, but he has got what he came for—'

'The Rocking P.'

Maria nodded. 'It was mine by right, I sold it to the Murphy sisters, and I am convinced Gonzales has taken it from them – perhaps left them a token payment.' She shrugged. 'However, he has it, and he will be satisfied. But in the past day or so we have become aware that two men from Pueblito have been shadowing us – and it is of those men that we are afraid.'

'Troublemakers,' Garcia said.

Maria nodded quickly. 'Luis Delgado is growing old now, but he has killed before today, with knife and gun, and got away with it. Herrera – he is a waster, a man with no backbone – but together, those two, they are dangerous. That they are following us can be for but one reason: they know why we are here, and they plan to rob us.'

'They knew you were about to inherit a ranch? Knew you were riding to Texas to sell it?'

Garcia smiled sadly. 'The Laredo newspapers regularly reach Pueblito. Your father's death was big news. Names were mentioned, villagers easily put two and two together. . . .'

'So what do you want me to do?'

The question was put so bluntly it caused Maria to bite her lip. Her lemonade glass was empty. She looked down at it, touched the rim with the tip of a finger. Then she took a deep breath. She shook her head, and cast a desperate sideways glance at her father.

Garcia said stiffly, 'Warren, your mother wishes you to ride with her to the Bravo. She is not in any way suggesting that it is your duty to protect her, and she will understand perfectly if you cannot find it in your heart—'

'For God's sake,' Warren said wearily. 'The woman I have known as my mother since I was old enough to recognize her face and her voice and the scent of her body is in Bigfoot being questioned by the town marshal. He believes she arranged the murder of her husband. That murder dropped the Rocking P in your lap. Now you expect – no, now you are *blackmailing* me into abandoning her. You want me to drop everything, saddle up and act as unpaid bodyguard to protect you from two bandits—'

'Not bandits.'

'As good as.' Warren glared at Garcia. 'What about you? Can't you protect your daughter?'

'If I were twenty years younger—'

'Christ,' Warren said feelingly, 'is there no end to it? I suppose next you'll be telling me you recently lost your wife. . . .'

He saw the stricken look on Garcia's face, and closed his eyes in the sudden awful silence.

After a moment Warren straightened in his chair and looked at Garcia.

'I'm sorry. That was unforgivable. I'm impatient, I'm cranky, I'm unbearably rude; I'm . . . I'm not myself. But just as I'm expected to understand your situation, so you must try to understand mine. Rocking P has been my home for more than twenty years – as far as I knew, that was all of my life, then suddenly I discovered I was a year older than that and my mother—' He pulled a face. 'Anyway, in a matter of days, it's been taken from us; from me, and

110

from Rosie.'

'If only the money had been in your account,' Maria said, 'it could have been so different. It would not have mattered to me who bought the ranch.'

'But it wasn't there,' Warren said. 'We didn't have it, Clayton T. had been running Rocking P badly. . . .' He hesitated, drummed his fingers on the table, then banged it with his fist.

'It's what, a hundred miles to the Bravo? No more than a week, there and back. OK, I'll do it; I'll go with you.'

'Warren, Warren,' Maria said softly.

And suddenly Warren grinned.

'It's your eyes,' he said. 'All the talk in the world couldn't sway me, but when you look at me with those eyes. . . .'

'Then I will try to restrict myself to just the occasional look at my son,' Maria said, her smile dazzling, 'otherwise who knows what I might persuade you to do?'

'There you go again,' Warren said, feeling his heart lurch. '*My son.* You know, the more you say that, the more I like it; it's something I could very easily become accustomed to.'

THIRTEEN

It was late afternoon when Warren Pallister, Maria and her father rode out of Rocking P and took the trail north into Bigfoot. Dark clouds were gathering, their swollen shapes blotting out the sun. The wind was rattling the trees, and the air was heavy with the scent of rain.

By making for Bigfoot they were heading in the wrong direction for travellers planning to cross the Bravo at Laredo, but the distance out of their way was short and Warren was deeply worried about his mother. He had answered the Mexicans' questions about her predicament with a measure of confidence, and agreed to act as escort, but he knew that he would break that promise without a qualm if Rosie was in trouble.

Before leaving the ranch, Warren walked quickly across the yard to the bunkhouse. He told Furnival, Rickard and Park that the Rocking P had been sold to Meg and Sinéad Murphy, but that a landowner from across the Mexican border was causing trouble. It was possible, he told them, that the Mexican had acquired Rocking P for himself by flavouring hard cash with extreme violence. If that was true, then the Mexican – a certain Señor Gonzales – would almost certainly descend on Rocking P.

With a grin, Furnival informed Warren that they would treat the Mexican with every courtesy – at which Bony Park spat musically into the cuspidor kept especially for him, and Al Rickard turned deliberately to his locker and from it took his gun-belt and well-worn six-gun.

On the ride into town there was very little talk. Maria was nervous, her face pale, Garcia, grim-faced but phlegmatic. His eyes were watchful, but in Warren's opinion there would be no trouble until they were well clear of Bigfoot and on their way south-west.

His prediction was correct, for they made it all the way into town without encountering any problems. Warren led the way past Alex Crow's office and the livery barn with its tilted windmill to the jail, where they tied their horses. Then, suggesting to Maria and Garcia that they eat a good meal at Caroline's café – which could be their last for some time – and watching them walk wearily up the street, he went inside to talk to Brent Coolidge.

'To tell you the truth,' Brent Coolidge said, 'this whole business developing out of, or existing prior

113

to, Clayton T.'s murder has got so damn complicated I'm pretty sure Rosie's been used. There's a tricky Mex been living with the Murphys – could be a killer; another Mex arrives and turns out to be your real mother; then, dang me if another *three* don't ride into town looking like bad trouble. So, with all that going on – and because technically Rocking P's no longer Rosie's home – I've got her settled in the rooming house.'

Warren leaned back in the hard chair and took a deep, relieved breath.

'In that case, I'm sorry I didn't offer you a drink earlier.'

Coolidge grinned. 'Lawmen are used to being glared at from the end of people's uptilted noses. Goes with the job.' He cocked an eyebrow. 'Is that all you called in for, news of Rosie, or have you got something for me?'

'Maria's carrying a lot of cash. They've spotted two men from their village, Pueblito. They must have followed Maria and her father here, and there can be only one reason for that: they're after the money. Maria is frightened, and her father is old. She's asked me to escort her to the border, and I've agreed.'

'Seeing as she's your real mother,' Coolidge said, 'you couldn't very well refuse.' His eyes were sympathetic. 'You're a young feller. This whole business must be tyin' you in knots. Finding Maria's one thing, but it's not every day a man loses his home and the woman he always *believed* was his ma.'

'Being young makes it easier for me to handle trouble; the same can't be said for the Murphys.'

Coolidge frowned.

'What about 'em? They've just bought a ranch. A straightforward deal. Or am I looking on the bright side? I know that woman Maria warned me about what *might* happen, but are you saying those greasers *did* ride out there to join their pal, Chavez?'

'They did, and they caused trouble. Maria and her father were riding out of the Murphy place when Gonzales and his men turned up. They were forced to hide in the woods. They heard some talk – not a lot. It was followed by the sound of a shot, probably from a shotgun. Then a woman screamed.'

'Conclusions?'

'Inside that house, someone was hurt. And Gonzales has got his hands on the Rocking P.'

'No prizes for guessing where he'll go next.'

'He'll want to view his acquisition,' Warren said drily. 'I've warned the hands.'

'Should've warned 'em not to resist.'

'Same answer: like me, they're grown men and can deal with trouble. It's Meg and Sinéad Murphy you should be worried about.'

'And I'll throw your answer right back at you: I was dealing with trouble when you were a twinkle in Clayton T.'s eye. Soon's I get through talking to you, I'll ride out there.'

Warren stood up.

'I'm finished,' he said. 'Maria and her father are

eating. I'm about to do the same.' He hesitated. 'There was a lot of talk in Alex Crow's office about legality and formalities and such like. I don't think a man like Gonzales will be too concerned about doing things right, but he will want proof of ownership. He'll have made sure he's got a bill of sale. Now he'll want the Rocking P deeds – and they're in Alex Crow's safe.'

The first spots of rain were dimpling the dust of Bigfoot's wide street when, from behind the rickety windmill in front of the livery barn, Luis Delgado and Pepe Herrera watched the three riders unhitch their horses from the rail in front of Brent Coolidge's jail and point their heads towards the south-west.

Thunder rumbled in the distance. Lightning flickered against the black skies, and Herrera cursed softly under his breath and began unrolling his slicker.

He said, 'The presence of Warren Pallister makes snatching the money much more difficult.'

Delgado snorted. 'Your fears are unfounded. Before we were faced by one old man, and a woman we can ignore in terms of fighting qualities. One young man is not enough to swing the balance of power their way.'

'Young men are fast and strong. He could prove dangerous.'

'He could be a minor irritation, but that is all – and in any case, circumstances are working in our favour. You are complaining about the weather, but the weather will wreck their concentration and conceal our approach. We will attack them out of the rain, and we will do it at night.'

'Guided by their camp-fire around which they will be huddled in their acute discomfort,' Herrera said. 'And of course, there will be no moon.'

'The moon will be there, as always,' Delgado said, smiling, 'but like us it will be well hidden.'

'And you remember what we discussed?'

'About seeing what develops, when the time comes?'

Herrera nodded. 'Just that. And nothing has changed except that the time is almost upon us and now there is one more person who, if allowed, would be capable of telling tales.'

'One person, six persons. . . .' Delgado snapped his fingers dismissively. 'The numbers do not matter. Nobody will tell tales,' he said, gazing off almost hungrily into the dark distance, 'because, when this night is finished, there will be nobody left alive.'

FOURTEEN

For Gonzales it was the end of a long trail and so excitement was blazing in his dark eyes and he was sitting proudly erect in the saddle as he led Rubio and Blanco on to the land that was the Rocking P. In the gloom of a stormy dusk the shingle roof of the house glistened with rain. No light gleamed in the windows.

'That is something to be thankful for,' Gonzales said, swinging out of the saddle. 'There is nobody to question my right to be here, to enter the house, to make myself at home.'

'I wouldn't be too sure of that,' Blanco said. He and Rubio had also dismounted. Both men were fingering their six-guns and looking away from Gonzales.

Gonzales swung around.

Three men were crossing the yard.

One man was limping. Another was moving as if lacking in strength. The third, in Gonzales' opinion, looked too old to be moving at all.

All three were armed.

With a muttered command, Gonzales brushed past his two gunmen. He dipped two fingers into his pocket and found the bill of sale. With that in his hand he walked to meet the three men. They met in the middle of the yard.

'My name's Furnival,' the limping man said.

'You are the foreman? The ramrod? The strawboss?'

'In the absence of the genuine article, I'm all of those,' Furnival said, eyes glinting with amusement. 'How about you, feller? D'you have business here? Because, if so, I can tell you that almost everyone's away on fall round-up.'

'The business I have here,' Gonzales said, 'is to look over this property which I have today purchased.'

'Oh yeah? Who from?'

'From the Murphy sisters.'

'And where'd they get it?'

'Earlier today they bought it from Maria Pallister, who inherited the property upon the death of her husband, Clayton T. Pallister.'

'Shucks, and here's me believing *Rosie* was married to Clayton. OK, so if Meg and Sinéad just bought the Rocking P, why'd they sell it to you?'

'They . . . reconsidered.'

'And you just happened to be there?' Furnival looked over Gonzales' shoulder. 'Backed up by those two ugly specimens?'

'It is a long and dangerous ride from Mexico, and I was carrying a large sum of money. In those circumstances it was wise to bring bodyguards.'

'From two nice old ladies, protection's the last thing you needed. What I can understand is you bringing along a show of force so's you get what you set out for. Is that the way it went? You made your offer, it was refused, so your two hard men got rough?'

Gonzales smiled. Furnival made a big show of looking about him.

'As a matter of interest,' he said, 'where's Raulo Chavez?'

'Ah, yes,' Gonzales said softly. 'Sadly, Raulo met with an accident and could not be with us.'

Bony Park cleared his throat, and spat.

'I did hear tell that wily old bird Sinéad Murphy kept a shotgun hid away. That wouldn't be the accident Chavez met with – would it now?'

Gonzales shook his head impatiently.

'These questions and unfounded accusations are a waste of my valuable time—'

'His valuable time,' Al Rickard said in marvelling tones, and he glanced in mock amazement at Park.'

'—and totally unnecessary because I have here a bill of sale signed by all the parties concerned.'

He held it out. Furnival took it, glanced through it.

'Show them all,' Gonzales said.

'Al's not interested in much just now. Bony can't read his own name.' Furnival squinted at Gonzales. 'Those Murphy signatures look shaky.'

'As you said, they are old women.'

'Both of them write a bit for the local newspaper. Short pieces, local interest, but for that kind of work they need clear writing.'

'They had been involved in delicate financial negotiations, twice in one day. I believe they were feeling the strain.'

'Like you pointed out,' Furnival said, handing back the bill of sale, 'questions and unfounded accusations are getting us nowhere. So I'll get straight to the point. A bill of sale's not worth the paper it's written on. You can stay here, on Rocking P land, but until I see the deeds to this property in your hot little hands, you're here on sufferance.'

'Sufferance?'

Furnival grinned. 'It means I'm allowing you to remain here, but with reluctance; I'm quite prepared to kick you off this land if I don't get that ultimate proof of ownership.'

'And where are those deeds, that proof I need? With the bank, perhaps, or—?'

'With the family's lawyer. You'll find he's a tough nut to crack.'

'And what about you men? You yourself, you look . . . competent. But your *compañeros* are insignificant. I see a man who looks very sick, another who is nearing the end of what has probably been a useless existence. With such a weak force at your disposal, do you seriously believe you could kick us off this land if that proof is not forthcoming?'

'Probably not,' Furnival said, ignoring Park's muttered string of oaths and standing fast with arms braced as the old wrangler tried to get at Gonzales. 'But if you're still here ten days from now, you'll find yourself facing foreman Jack Fisher returning from the fall round-up with thirty or more work-hardened cowpokes. If that bunch gets a-hold of you, you'll be riding out of here on a rail.'

The room was in darkness. Blanco located an oil lamp, ignited a lucifer with a flick of his thumbnail and applied it to the wick. Immediately, the warm glow drove back the shadows. Looking around, Gonzales noted the damaged table, the broken window, the big wagon wheel leaning against the wall and the frayed rope directly over the table from which it had hung.

Speaking in Spanish, he said, 'Raulo made a mess in here, with that tricky shot.'

'But what he did got you the ranch,' Blanco said, relaxed and comfortable in his own language.

'I'm sure for that he will go to Heaven,' Gonzales said drily. 'You know, that cowboy Furnival, he had a point. Until I get my hands on those deeds, my purchase of this ranch can be disputed.'

'Let people dispute,' Blanco said. 'Those two women have accepted your payment, and signed the bill of sale. They have also witnessed at close hand the extremes to which you will go to get what you want. If the sale is contested, those women will be rushing to confirm everything you say.'

'Out of fear?'

'That, yes – and something else,' Rubio said, joining the discussion. 'There is the matter of Raulo Chavez's death. He was killed by a fearsome blast from a shotgun. There was no more gunplay, in the room or outside; that shot was the only one fired, and it was fired by one of those old women. It is another thing we can hold over their heads: you get their co-operation, or we convince the law in Bigfoot that we witnessed cold-blooded murder.'

'Rubio, the clever one,' Gonzales said, winking at Blanco. 'But he is right, of course, and that threat is another weapon in our armoury.'

'So, what now?' Rubio said.

Gonzales was watching Blanco. He had wandered away, and now he glanced over his shoulder, grinning, as he discovered the late Clayton T. Pallister's supply of alcohol. Glasses clinked as he splashed whiskey into three crystal glasses. He carried them over to the table, liberally sprinkling the Persian carpet on the way.

'What now?' Gonzales echoed, rolling a sip of the expensive whiskey around his mouth and nodding his satisfaction. 'Now we do what the cowboy suggested. We ride into town, we find the lawyer holding the deeds—'

'It will be easy, for there is only one,' Blanco said. 'I have seen his brass shingle. I will take you to him.'

'So we go to that man,' Gonzales said, nodding approval, 'and we persuade—'

'Persuade?' Rubio said, grinning at Blanco.

'By whatever means are necessary,' Gonzales said.

'The Rocking P deeds will be in an iron safe,' Rubio said.

'The lawyer,' Blanco offered, 'will consider them to be secure there. Out of our reach.'

'Despite what they believe,' Gonzales said, 'lawyers are often wrong. Drink up your whiskey, we have some riding and some persuading to do.'

FIFTEEN

Although Brent Coolidge was determined to ride to the Murphy homestead as soon as he could, he knew his age was slowing him down and severely reducing his prowess with guns and fists. Sure, he and Warren Pallister had decided Gonzales and his crew would head for the Rocking P after settling with the Murphy sisters. But on the off chance that the Mexicans had hung around on the sisters' homestead, Coolidge thought it prudent to take help with him.

With that decision made, he was stopped on his way out of his office by memories of what Warren Pallister had said. Coolidge knew the youngster was right: Gonzales would need those deeds to the Rocking P, and without doubt he would come after them. But when?

Standing in the doorway and taking a quick look at the worsening weather, Coolidge came to a quick decision: Gonzales would move to get his hands on the deeds, but he was not in a hurry. He had the ranch to himself except for the skeleton staff Jack Fisher had left behind, and Coolidge was damn sure a man of his standing wouldn't ride into town in the middle of the night, in bad weather, simply to do something that could be done the next day.

With that decision made, Coolidge finally left his office. The only person he could turn to for help was part-time deputy George Gelert. George lived in a room over Barney Kay's saloon. By the time Coolidge had walked up the street – hugging the front of the buildings to keep out of the driving wind and rain – Warren and his Mexican charges had been gone a full hour.

It was almost another hour before a soaking wet Coolidge and George Gelert rode out of the trees and down the slope to the Murphys' homestead. The sight that met their eyes took both men completely by surprise, and gave dreamer George Gelert another rich source of tales to tell around the camp-fires.

Flickering oil lamps were swinging from trees, from timber uprights doing their damnedest to support the gallery's sagging overhang, and from the iron hoops over which a rickety old buckboard's canvas cover was stretched. By that dancing light and the occasional flash of lightning, Meg and Sinéad Murphy were loading their worldly possessions on to the buckboard and the shining top-buggy which was standing nearby. Like Coolidge and Gelert, they were dripping wet. Their long skirts clung wetly to their legs. Grey hair, tossed into disarray by wind and rain, plastered their faces and had constantly to be swept aside.

Meg was working with difficulty: her left wrist was heavily bandaged.

'Go look in the house,' she called when she saw the two riders and recognized Coolidge. 'There's a dead man there. Sinéad damn near blew his head off with her hideaway shotgun.'

Coolidge knew Raulo Chavez by sight, but it was with difficulty that he identified the body lying against the wall in the Murphys' living-room, because a face was something Chavez, in death, no longer possessed.

'Short range, both barrels,' George Gelert commented, in a clogged voice, and he quickly left the room. Idly listening to his deputy being violently sick, Coolidge wandered about the room picking up this and that and trying to get a sense of the explosive violence that still hung about the room in the form of lingering gunsmoke. But, other than that, the gruesome corpse was the only evidence. Sighing, Coolidge paused in his wandering and stood with hands on hips. It was, he reflected, a pretty pass when a landowner from Mexico could cross the border with a couple of gunslingers and force two harmless old ladies out of their home.

And then he was forced to smile: if he could speak, Raulo Chavez would object strongly to *harmless* as

127

being an apt description of the Murphy sisters.

Outside again, he saw Gelert hanging limply on the gallery's rail. The pale-faced part-time deputy was being buffeted by the wind. Lashing rain was soaking his bare head. Meg and Sinéad were metaphorically dusting off their hands: they'd finished packing, and were preparing to leave.

'Is all this necessary?' Coolidge said, clumping down the steps and ducking his head against the rain as he splashed through shallow pools to where the sisters were standing up against the buckboard. 'I've a fair idea of what's been going on with you and the Rocking P: you bought it from Maria Pallister, then this feller Gonzales turned up. If he used violence to take that ranch from you, the law can step in.'

'Oh, there was violence,' Meg said, 'but the only death is on his side and that dead man's in our living-room. If we start fighting, he could get us put away for murder.'

'Besides,' Sinéad said, 'Gonzales paid us in cash, so doesn't that make the sale legal?'

'Not if there was coercion.' Dashing rainwater from his face as he huddled under the scant shelter of the buckboard's canvas, Coolidge was looking shrewdly at the sisters. 'You didn't get back what you'd paid out, did you?'

Sinéad pulled a face. 'Maybe not, but there's no law against a man doing some hard bargaining.'

'I'm pretty sure Alex Crow could dig up a legal

precedent that'd show you've got just cause to fight the deal.'

'But we don't want to, Brent,' Meg said sweetly. 'We were taken in by that Chavez, went ahead and bought Rocking P and suddenly everything blew up in our faces. That suggests we're a couple of gullible old fools.'

'Running away may not help; there are rogues everywhere,' Coolidge said. He pursed his lips, muttered a silent oath as the wind pushed him against the tailgate. 'I take it you're going back East?'

'Buckboard and top-buggy to San Antonio. Then we sell them and take the railroad. And we're not running,' Meg said with a grin, 'we're beating a tactical retreat to familiar territory.'

'To fight another day?'

'You betcha.'

'Got enough cash?'

'Mind your own damn business, Brent Coolidge.'

'Are you in a hurry?'

'We're loaded and ready to go. Why, what did you have in mind?'

Coolidge waved an arm at the weather. 'You've got covered wagons, me and George, we've got horses. I'm not saying this storm's going to slacken, but a cup of hot coffee would set us up nicely for the ride into town.'

'Just supposing,' Sinéad said, 'we've got something in there we can heat water in, and can stand another sight of that dead body.'

'So have you, and can you?'

'We've left behind a couple of pots that weren't worth the bother of taking with us; we don't have to look at Raulo.'

'Then why don't we step inside out of the rain and enjoy a farewell drink?' Brent Coolidge said. 'You're in no hurry to be off, and I know for sure nothing's going to happen in Bigfoot until tomorrow morning at the earliest.'

SIXTEEN

Five miles to the south-west of Bigfoot, Delgado and Herrera were pushing their horses hard through the wind and driving rain. They had ridden out of town no more than ten minutes after Warren Pallister, Maria, and Santiago Garcia. Arguably that put them too close, but if they allowed any more time and distance to come between them, Herrera had said, they would risk losing their quarry.

From the outset there had been little chance of that. Although the muddy trail meandered through thickly wooded, hilly terrain, flashes of lightning regularly revealed ahead of them the three riders making across country on the long trek to the Bravo. Those brief glimpses through sheets of driving rain were enough to convince the two men riding in pursuit that they were unlikely to be seen: Warren Pallister might have been recruited as escort, but in the stormy weather he was likely to be far more use as a guide.

Nevertheless, it was the older man, Delgado, who suggested they ride hard to narrow the distance between them. He pointed out that, in the conditions, Pallister could call a halt at any time. If they were too far back and the riders they were chasing slipped into the thick woods, then indeed they could lose them – even if only for a short time.

His prophecy almost came true.

One brilliant flash of lightning that lit up the swollen skies revealed a solitary rider less than 400 yards ahead of them on the slick trail. Before the lightning flash had faded to a dull red glow on the retina, that rider had disappeared.

'He was on the edge of the woods,' Herrera said, drawing his horse to a halt at the edge of the dripping trees. 'If he has gone, he has slipped *into* the woods. They have had enough. Like us they are wet, cold, and miserable, sick of their horses slipping and sliding in the mud. They will make camp, light a fire and bed down for the night.'

'For us, the fire will be a beacon,' Delgado said. 'For them it will be a hypnotic source of heat that will hold their attention. In addition, there is the roar of the wind, the clatter of trees, the hiss of rain. All those sounds will mask the noise of our approach. An army could ride in on them, *muchos soldados*, and in these conditions they would be unaware.'

'I agree. Given the advantages we have, we two are as powerful as an army,' Herrera said.

Beneath the dripping sombrero, his face glistened

wet. Even in the darkness the silver conchos he wore for ornamentation gleamed as he moved restlessly.

'It was always going to be easy, but now it will be child's play,' the lean Delgado said. 'We can take them when and how we choose, with gun or with knife. They will not know what hit them; when it is finished, nobody will ever find their bodies where they lie mouldering under the leaves.'

'And nobody will find us,' Herrera said, his white teeth flashing as he grinned. 'Us: you, me, and all that money.'

'Come,' Delgado said, impatiently flicking his horse's reins and moving off. 'This that we are about to do will be doubly rewarding. Killing is always to be savoured; tonight, guided to our prey by the glow of a fire, we will be getting paid for doing something we enjoy.'

After much crashing and swearing in the dark, Warren Pallister and the two Mexicans came across a small clearing in the woods that yet provided enough cover to shield them from the worst of the wind. It was, Warren decided, better than taking cover under the thickest of the trees, where the rainwater collected by the dense canopy of leaves would be deposited on them in a drenching deluge by each gusting squall.

In that clearing they hobbled the horses and scavenged hurriedly to find enough dry wood to build a fire. Around it as it crackled and hissed they sat on logs, in a tight circle. Huddled under shining slickers, clutching tin cups of scalding hot coffee, they felt their eyelids drooping as their clothes steamed and the fire's heat soaked into chilled bodies.

'If those two men from your village are following us,' Warren said after a while, 'I can't see them making a move on a night like this. Nevertheless, if we're staying here until dawn we'll need to post a sentry. Two sleep, one stands watch. Maria, you're excused; your father and I will take turns.' He looked across the fire at Garcia. 'When the time comes, I'll take first watch. Wake me after two hours.'

'My eyes and ears are as good as any man's,' Maria said. 'It is silly to let me sleep.'

She was holding close to her the bulky linen bag given to her by Meg Murphy. She had been clinging to it as a mother would to a baby, never letting it out of her sight.

'Decision's made, we watch, you get your rest,' Warren said flatly, and he felt Maria's huge dark eyes on him as he drained his cup.

'The man on guard will need to be alert,' Garcia said. 'In normal circumstances the cracking of a twig in the night would awaken the weariest of men sleeping rough. But tonight there is too much noise created by the forces of nature.'

'All the more reason for camping out in the open,' Warren said. 'We're surrounded by open space – though not as much as I'd like – and they have to cross that to reach us.'

'They do not need to reach us,' Garcia said gloomily. 'A good man with a rifle could drop us all from a distance.'

'One of us,' Warren corrected. 'He would need to be very good indeed to down all three of us—'

The crack of a rifle cut him short. The muzzle flash winked red on the edge of the clearing. There was a solid thump as the bullet hit home. Maria grunted low in her throat and sagged towards the fire. Gritting his teeth, Warren leaped towards her. With one hand he pushed her sideways so that she fell away from the flames. Agony flared as the sudden movement tore at his injured shoulder. A second shot cracked. The bullet whined wickedly over Warren's head. He rolled forward, regained his feet, glanced once at Maria's recumbent form then began a crouching run for the deep shadows under the trees.

A third shot tore across the clearing as he neared the woods. From close to the fire he heard the rattle of gunfire. He tumbled into the trees, tugged out his pistol and glanced back. Garcia was kneeling by Maria. His six-gun was in his hand. He was blazing away at the rifleman's position. Then the pistol's hammer clicked on an empty chamber. Without hesitation the lean Mexican spun away from his daughter and ran. Warren grinned savagely as he watched the wily old man run for the *opposite* side of the clearing. Garcia had thought coolly under fire.

The gunman now had two targets, widely separated. He'd also lost the advantage of surprise.

But, according to Garcia, two troublemakers had followed them from Pueblito. So, where was the second of those men?

Huddled down in the shadows, Warren could see Maria lying ominously still. The fire cast a weak circle of light that fell far short of the trees. The wind, like the rain now perceptibly slackening, still moaned eerily through the uppermost branches. It was impossible to hear movement. There was also no way of communicating with Santiago Garcia.

The clearing was encircled by the woods. Just inside the timber, Warren was down on one knee. Rainwater from the trees was again soaking his clothing. Flicking water from his eyes he risked poking his head forward. Flesh creeping in anticipation of a bullet, he squinted through the trees to his left.

He estimated that the rifleman who had gunned down Maria was in the woods no more than thirty yards away. Garcia was in the woods the same distance away on the rifleman's other side. The second man could be anywhere – discount him, Warren thought; go after the known, not the unknown, but always with the realization that a killing shot could come from anywhere.

Dragging his sleeve across his wet face, he began inching his way through the trees. He moved in a cramped crouch, frequently supporting himself with his hands. Progressing soundlessly was impossible. Undergrowth crackled beneath his boots, beneath his knees. Branches clung to his clothing, then jerked free with sharp snaps. But the sound of the wind was ever present. Under cover of its eerie moaning and the whip and crack of wildly tossing branches, Warren clawed his way ever closer to the gunman's position. *Or,* he corrected, *to where I believe him to be.*

After a few minutes he was forced to stop. His breathing was ragged; his legs cramped; his injured shoulder on fire. He looked to his right, towards the fire. Maria had not moved. Fearing the worst, Warren closed his eyes. When he opened them, still looking across the clearing, he saw movement in the trees.

Damn it, Garcia, stay down, was his immediate wild thought. And then, as the Mexican stood up and deliberately stepped clear of the woods and into the open with his six-gun not in his hand, but pouched, Warren realized what he was doing.

He must have been watching me, Warren thought. *He saw me edging towards where we believe the gunman to be lying low, knows I'm close — and he's offering himself as a target; he's drawing the gunman's fire.*

Tense, barely able to breathe for the tight band around his chest, Warren stayed down in the soaking undergrowth, watching, waiting. He saw Garcia draw himself to his full height; saw, even across the clearing and by the meagre, flickering light of the fire, Garcia's eyes constantly darting from Warren's position to the recumbent figure of his daughter.

This is for her, for Maria, Warren thought. *He is exposing himself to draw fire because he wants me to finish this, and I cannot finish it until the gunman, in his turn, exposes himself. He wants this over so he can cross the clearing to his daughter.*

Yet even as Warren was thinking those thoughts, the waiting became too much for Garcia. From the daring, confrontational stance on the edge of the woods he seemed to wilt, as if in surrender. Then he exploded into movement. He broke into a run. His hand snapped down. He drew his six-gun. Running for the camp-fire, he snapped wild shots at the woods – so wild that Warren was forced to duck even lower as the Mexican's bullets whined dangerously close to his own position.

Then the rifleman broke his long silence. A single shot cracked out. Closing in on the camp-fire, Garcia took the bullet from the rifle in his upper body. He took two more loping strides. Then his legs buckled. He fell flat on his face. His six-gun flew from his hand, skidding skidded across the wet grass. It came to rest in the blackened embers at the edge of the camp-fire.

Santiago Garcia lay still.

He was down, possibly finished, but he had done his job. The rifle's muzzle flash had pinpointed the gunman's position for Warren; he was startled to discover he was almost close enough to stretch out an arm and touch him. And once the man's position was revealed, as if by magic his shape became visible: he was a dark, clearly defined bulk on the other side of squat bushes tossing wildly in the wind.

Carefully, still kneeling, Warren rested the barrel of his six-gun on his forearm. He squeezed the trigger, fired one steady shot aimed for the centre of that dark shape. He heard a muffled cry of shock and pain. For a moment nothing happened. Then the dark shape went down; it was there, then gone. Beyond the tossing bushes, there was no sound, no movement. The rifleman was finished.

That one was for Garcia, Warren thought.

Then the downed man's partner, the second gunman from Pueblito, entered the fray.

A fusillade of shots sent twigs flying and rainwater showering down on Warren. From the woods on the other side of the clearing – remarkably close to where Garcia had been standing – that second man burst forth. He was a savage figure in the fading glow from the fire. A sombrero shaded the gaunt face of an ageing man, but the pistol blazing in his hand made him as dangerous as a vigorous young man with sharp eyes and fire in his veins. As Warren snapped a quick shot, and missed, he ran directly for the fire. There he threw himself down, and now he had an advantage: he was using as a shield the motionless bodies of Maria and Santiago Garcia.

Mexican stand-off, Warren thought – and grinned mirthlessly.

'Who are you?' he called.

'I am Luis Delgado.' A pause. 'Is Herrera dead?'

'Probably.'

'And perhaps also Garcia, and his daughter – in which case it is you and me.'

'If you walk away,' Warren said, 'it's just me.'

Delgado chuckled.

'I am too close to what we came for,' he said, and he stretched out his left hand and touched the bulky linen bag lying close to Maria.

'Being close gets you nothing,' Warren said. 'You can't spend that money in a clearing in the woods.'

'Is true,' Delgado said. 'So we come to an . . . arrangement.'

'Which brings us back to what I said: you get up, and you walk away – without that bag.'

'Is not possible.'

'It's the only way.'

Then, out of nowhere, two fast shots rang out. As a third followed, then a fourth, Delgado reared up. Puffs of ash rose from the fire. Delgado looked about him wildly.

Without compunction, Warren shot him in the chest. The Mexican went backwards as if hit by a bull. The big sombrero flew from his head. It was caught by the wind and, like a wagon-wheel leaving a broken axle, it rolled away across the clearing.

And that one was for me, from Garcia, Warren thought, rising to his feet. For the shots had come from Garcia's pistol: the heat of the fire had detonated the remaining bullets in the Mexican's pistol, and given Warren the few seconds he needed to finish the job.

SEVENTEEN

Maria was dead.

It was Santiago Garcia who made the pronounce-ment, down on his knees alongside his daughter, the cold rain thinning the blood soaking his shirt at the shoulder and falling like tears on Maria's pale, closed eyelids.

After watching Garcia rise groggily to his feet, Warren had quickly taken hold of Delgado's heels, dragged his body into the woods and dumped it alongside that of his partner, Herrera.

Now he was standing looking down at the grey-haired man and thinking that Garcia's loss was his loss, too, for Maria was his mother.

'No sooner found, than taken away,' he said quietly.

Garcia looked up quickly.

'Not found,' he said, shaking his head. 'Maria was not your mother.'

'But. . . .'

Warren felt as if all the wind had been knocked out of him. Yet even as the shock hit home, as sadness welled within him, instinct told him that those feelings would pass quickly. Maria had come into his life, but her stay there had been fleeting. He had been touched by her femininity, by her deep, soulful eyes, but he had not been in her presence for long enough to get to know her well. And, Warren realized with a jolt, if Maria never had been his mother, then he and Rosie had been the victims of a deception that had seen them evicted from the home that was still rightfully theirs.

'I'm beginning to understand,' he said, his voice hardening. 'You had the birth certificate, the marriage certificate, you showed them to Alex Crow—'

'And, of course, I also had two daughters,' Garcia cut in. 'The one called Maria married Clayton T. Pallister. She had her son snatched from her when her husband deserted her, and a year later she died of pneumonia.'

'And the woman I knew as Maria?'

'She is . . . was . . . Valentina, named for her mother, who died the day before we left Pueblito. She was Maria's twin sister. They were identical, and so those eyes that you thought you recognized because they were *your* eyes in a way truly were. If there was anything in the deception that was close to the truth, then surely it was that likeness.'

'Maybe,' Warren said, 'but in that deception there

was not a single morsel of truth. It was a plan conceived by . . . by you?'

'By me, yes. I had read the Laredo newspapers and learned of Clayton T.'s death. It came to me at once that if Valentina could pass herself off as her dead sister, Maria, then the second marriage would be bigamous and Rocking P would be ours. The morning we buried my wife, we set out for the Bravo.'

'To cross into Texas and take possession of, then sell, a ranch to which you had no legal claim.'

Garcia shrugged. He was still down on his knees. The strength was ebbing away from him; he was physically drained by his loss, and by the bullet wound in his shoulder. But, even in extremity, Warren noticed, he had his wits about him: he was holding tight to the linen bag containing the money he and his daughter had obtained by deceit.

Warren shook his head and sighed.

'One hell of a mess,' he said, sinking down on to a log and looking pensively at the wounded, grieving Mexican.

'It goes like this, doesn't it? You sold a ranch you didn't own to Meg and Sinéad Murphy, who were then forced to sell it to a man called Gonzales who now believes he owns Rocking P,' he said. 'Money has changed hands, Garcia, deals have been struck by people fighting over the ownership of a ranch that was not up for sale. And the big loser is Gonzales, right? The man at the end of the line. You got your money from the Murphys, and walked away. He paid

144

his money to the Murphys, and is probably already in residence at Rocking P. But by daylight tomorrow I will be back in Bigfoot. Before the morning's out, Alex Crow will have set matters straight and Gonzales will be out on his ear.'

He paused, thinking.

'In Crow's office, you said there was no death certificate, because Maria had not died. That was a lie. What about the certificate?'

Garcia patted his pocket. 'It was here, all the time.'

'I'll need it to prove Rosie's marriage to Clayton T. was legal.'

Without a word, Garcia took the crumpled paper from his pocket and handed it to Warren.

'Unfortunately,' he said, 'Jesus Gonzales will not accept being a loser.'

'The solution to that is simple,' Warren said. 'The people concerned return the money paid to them.'

'No.'

'Somehow,' Warren said, 'I expected that.' He hesitated. 'You're in no fit state to fight; you know I could force you to return with me and give the Murphys their money.'

'And they in turn would give Gonzales his?' Garcia shook his head. 'I know that, but somehow. . . .'

Warren nodded thoughtfully. 'On the other hand, perhaps we could come to an arrangement?'

'It is possible, yes.'

'Gonzales used violence against two frail ladies to get what he wanted. He deserves to lose his money –

145

but then we're back to the Murphys, and it's those sisters I feel for. They paid you a fair price. What about Gonzales? Would he have been fair to the sisters?'

Garcia managed a grim smile. 'You are joking, of course.'

'I suppose I am. So, what's your guess? What would he have paid Meg and Sinéad for Rocking P? Five per cent less than they gave you?'

'Ten per cent less,' Garcia said. 'At least.' And then, slowly, a smile of dawning understanding lit up his dark eyes. 'That is the arrangement I am to consider? From the money I have here, I give you ten per cent? You return to Bigfoot, and give that money to the Murphys?'

'Sound reasonable? That way, they come out even, Gonzales stays a loser and pays for his crimes of violence.'

'And me?'

'You win,' Warren said flatly. 'But that money you take back with you to Pueblito could turn out to be a kind of poisoned chalice. You've already said Gonzales won't accept being a loser. It won't take him long to work out that the easiest way of getting his money back is to talk to his neighbour in Mexico. That's you.'

'No matter,' Garcia said smoothly. 'The money will be safe. A way of ensuring that was worked out on the day my plan was conceived.'

'You can handle Gonzales?'

146

'The way it has been arranged, I will have no need to handle him, or anyone else, because the money will be safe,' Garcia said simply. He looked hard at Warren. 'We have a deal?'

Silently, Warren extended his hand. Garcia took it. They shook hands sombrely.

'I know Maria will go back to Pueblito with you,' Warren said quietly as he rose from the log, 'but that still leaves us with some grave digging to do.'

'The earth is wet and soft,' Santiago Garcia said. 'Together, with your strength and my feeble help, we will dig two graves. And then, afterwards, the arrangement will be settled when the sum of ten per cent changes hands.'

EIGHTEEN

It was still dark and raining hard when Gonzales rode into Bigfoot ahead of Rubio and Blanco, but the Mexican landowner's concern was not for the weather. With every hour that passed he was more convinced than ever that the Rocking P deeds should be in his possession, so it was with considerable impatience that he watched Blanco swing his horse over to the right of the street and ride close to the plank walk, looking at doors.

Then, in silence, the man with pale eyes drew his horse to a halt, swung from the saddle and waved the others over.

'Here,' Blanco said quietly as they joined him and dismounted. 'This brass plate is the one I remember.'

'What we hope now,' Gonzales said, reading the name, 'is that this Alex Crow sleeps over the office.'

'I will quietly persuade the door to let us in,' Rubio said, grinning.

148

He stepped forward, and did something with the butt of his six-gun. With the faintest splintering of wood, the door swung open. Now taking up the rear, Gonzales followed Rubio and Blanco inside. The office was in darkness. It smelled richly of leather. The faint light seeping in from the street's oil lamps revealed the front of a desk, bookshelves, a door at the rear. Brass hinges emitted an oily sigh as they went through that second door. Ahead of them, a flight of stairs led into darkness.

Then they were halted in their tracks.

'What the hell do you two want?'

The voice, coming from behind them, stunned Gonzales and sent a shiver down his spine. He closed his eyes, then turned slowly. A short fat man with a bald head that shone like a wooden Indian's in the gloom was pointing a derringer at his head.

'We are looking for Alex Crow,' Gonzales said ingratiatingly. 'Our business is of great importance. There was no answer to our knock—'

'There was no knock. I worked late, fell asleep at my desk as I often do. The first thing I knew was when I awoke and saw you two creeping through.'

You two, Gonzales noted. Not *you three*. He gestured silently to Rubio, who had led the way deeper into the building, then nodded to Blanco and together they returned to the office. Deliberately, Gonzales moved very close to the still open front door. To keep the derringer trained on the two men, Crow was forced to turn his back to the inner door.

149

'Perhaps, not wanting to disturb others, we knocked too softly,' Gonzales said. 'But although important to me, we are here on a simple matter that should not keep you much longer from your bed. I have purchased the Rocking P. To complete the deal I need the deeds.'

'Come back in office hours.'

'That is not reasonable. Morning approaches, and we are here now. It is a simple matter of turning a key in a lock.'

Crow shook his head. 'Sorry. You're intruders who broke into my office, and now I must ask you to leave—'

His words were cut short. Silently, Rubio had crept up behind him. Suddenly what felt like a band of iron encircled the lawyer's neck. It tightened on his throat. He dropped the derringer and clawed desperately at the arm that threatened cruelly to strangle him.

Rubio laughed softly. Clenching his fist, he tightened the choke hold.

'So now we have a very different situation,' Gonzales said smoothly. 'It seems that office hours have been moved forward, for now you will open the safe.'

Then he too broke off as the clatter of horse's hoofs drew rapidly nearer, terminated suddenly, and boots thudded on the plank walk.

Blanco flattened himself against the wall. Rubio dragged Crow back into the shadows. Gonzales turned to face the door.

Marshal Brent Coolidge appeared in the opening. His badge gleamed. He was outlined against the street's faint light. He saw Gonzales. Swiftly he drew his six-gun. There was a metallic click as the hammer snapped back.

'What the hell are you doing here—'

Blanco fired once.

The bullet spun Coolidge around. He banged against the door frame. The solid timber support kept him upright. Face twisted in shock, he snapped two shots. Dazzled by the muzzle flash, he was firing blind into the gloom of the office. Even so, he found the target. Blanco yelped, like a dog in pain. Then his breath was expelled in a long sigh. The sound was followed by the dull thud of a body falling.

Out of the corner of his eye, frozen in the cross-fire, Gonzales saw Blanco go down. Conscious of the marshal still on his feet, his gun menacing, he uttered a soft Spanish curse. Then he ran. Cringing in expectation of the next shot, he tried to squeeze his body into a narrow alcove alongside the bookshelves.

Rubio released Alex Crow. Roughly he pushed him so that the lawyer crashed against the wall and fell heavily. Then he dropped to a crouch behind the desk and went for his gun.

The blast of his shot coincided with the crack of Coolidge's Colt. Splinters flew from the door jamb. An ink-well shattered. Black liquid spattered

Gonzales. Rubio swore as a fragment of pottery gashed his cheek.

On the floor, breathing with difficulty, Alex Crow rolled out of the line of fire. He grimaced as the fallen derringer bored into his hip. He fumbled for it, lifted it high and pulled back the tiny hammer. Around the desk, through watering eyes, he could see the blurred outline of Rubio's bulk. Gunsmoke was clouding the air, stinging the nostrils. Coolidge and Rubio continued to exchange shots. At close range, they were firing wild. Bullets whanged off the oil lamp, thudded into thick volumes on the shelves.

Crow pulled the trigger.

Lost in the powerful roar of six-guns, the derringer's detonation was like the faint crack of an icicle breaking. The bullet, a particle of lead the size of birdshot, hit the Mexican in the right eye. It bored straight through, piercing his brain. He crumpled. Dead before he hit the ground, he lay in sudden, aching silence as all shooting ceased.

From the door, young Warren Pallister said, 'I don't know, I leave town for a few hours and all hell's let loose.'

NINETEEN

When dawn's early light painted the town of Bigfoot with its welcome warmth, the rain had ceased and the wind had dropped to a gentle breeze.

In Brent Coolidge's office, three men nursed various injuries.

Coolidge was leaning back in his swivel chair with his feet on the desk. The ageing marshal was wearing a stark white bandage like a badge of honour. The look on his face was one of genial smugness.

Above Alex Crow's collar, his neck was swollen purple. He was having difficulty swallowing, but as he gingerly sipped hot coffee his eyes, too, glowed with pride.

Warren Pallister's shoulder was healing well.

He said, 'So that death certificate sets everything right?'

'Definitely,' Crow said hoarsely. 'That, and the truly amazing story you've brought back with you.'

'He's an amazing man, Santiago Garcia. He saw

his chance, seized the opportunity. Once he got here, a heap of money sort of fell into his lap. Then other people's greed took over and things got chaotic.'

'Well, the other Mexican, Gonzales, is left to rue his folly and bury three of his henchmen.'

'I should arrest him,' Coolidge growled.

Crow shook his head. 'Don't bother. He's lost money, that's enough. And Warren and Rosie have got their ranch back.'

'Never lost it,' Warren said, shaking his head in disbelief.

There was silence for a few moments as each man pondered on the strange sequence of events that had hit the area since Clayton T. Pallister's death.

Eventually, Warren said, 'And you say the Murphys have left town?'

'Headed back East,' Coolidge confirmed.

Warren nodded slowly, 'Well,' he said, 'when we'd buried the two men from Pueblito, Santiago Garcia handed over to me ten per cent of what he got from the Murphys. I'm supposed to give it back to them to make up a shortfall, but with them gone. . . .'

'Shame to waste it,' Coolidge said.

Crow grinned.

'You thinking what I'm thinking?'

'We both are,' Warren said, rising from his chair. 'I'll cross the street, tell Mick over at the livery barn he'll get his new windmill after all.'

EPILOGUE

A week later, the sun was a molten disc in the searing white skies over Pueblito. Jesus Gonzales rode into the village at midday. Siesta time. The steep, stony street was deserted. In a small, rock-walled paddock, shaggy goats lifted their heads to watch his approach. A dog lying on its side in the middle of the street remained motionless as Gonzales's horse picked its way daintily over its recumbent form.

From the young woman from Pueblito who worked for him as a maid, Gonzales learned the location of Santiago Garcia's house. It was, he had been told, quite close to the cemetery where Garcia's wife was buried.

Of course, Gonzales expected to find several adobe cottages in that area, and had been anticipating some difficulty. He need not have worried. Santiago Garcia was expecting him. He had kept watch for several days. Now, as the sound of hoofs rang out in the stony street, he was in his doorway, waiting.

Gonzales pulled his weary horse to a halt. He slid from the saddle, slapped dust from his gloved hands, eased his sombrero off his wet brow.

'You know why I am here?'

'I know your journey is wasted.'

Gonzales's eyebrows lifted.

'Not at all. It is a simple matter. You have money that belongs to me. I want it back.'

'Two frail women in Texas have money that belongs to you. You should talk to them.'

'They have left Texas and are probably even now in New York. Besides, the fact that my money went to those two is a mere technicality. There were several transactions concerning the Rocking P, but just the one person emerged as loser. When you return the money to me, that will be put right.'

Without a word, Santiago Garcia took his hand from behind his back. He was holding the linen bag that had been passed to Maria by Meg Murphy. He tossed it to Gonzales.

Gonzales caught it with one hand. His lips tightened. He looked with curiosity and growing anger at Garcia.

'This bag is empty.'

'As I said, the ride from your hacienda was pointless, your time wasted.'

'If I do not get the money—'

'The money has been distributed,' Garcia said serenely, and he began to turn away. 'If you want

156

what you consider to be your money, then you must call on each family here and plead your case. You will need to talk to the heads of those families, for each of them has been given a small portion of the much larger sum that was in that bag.'

He smiled, watching with satisfaction as Gonzales's sweat-streaked face registered confusion, then growing consternation.

'I wish you luck,' Garcia said, 'just as those families wished me luck almost two weeks ago when Valentina and I left here to cross the Bravo, for my wronged dead daughter Maria, and most definitely for Pueblito.'